John P Brady was born in Dublin in 1980 and grew up in rural Ireland. He moved to London at the age of 18 before returning to Dublin where he spent a decade of his adult life. He studied at University College Dublin and the University of Pisa, Italy. He has worked as a teacher, translator, journalist, barman, stockroom clerk, roofer and musician. In 2011 he immigrated to Sicily to learn Italian and concentrate on writing fiction.

This is the first title by John P Brady.
He is currently searching for representation for his next project: a novel about life in Sicily which is complete.

Further information is available here:
www.johnpbrady.com
Please subscribe for updates

I0682910

Back to the Gaff

Scandalous Narratives of Contemporary Ireland

John P Brady

Roadside Fiction
Dublin, Ireland

First published by Roadside Fiction (Republic of Ireland) 2014
This edition 2018

Copyright © John P Brady 2014

www.roadsidefiction.com
www.johnpbrady.com

ISBN-13: 978-0-9929323-1-2
ISBN-10: 0992932319

Disclaimer:
This is a work of fiction. Names, characters, businesses, places, events and incidents are either the products of the author's imagination or used in a fictitious manner. Any resemblance to actual persons, living or dead, or actual events is purely coincidental.

This book would not have been possible without the policies of the Government of the Republic of Ireland, the Department of Education and Dublin City Council. As an Irish citizen, I feel proud to have been afforded the opportunity to return to university as a mature student.

Back to the Gaff

John P Brady

Introduction by the author

The stories in this book take place during some of the most important and formative periods of one's life: university, post-university freedom and exploration and early working life. They evoke the thoughts and frustrations, views and perversions of the youth of Ireland during the late-boom and post-boom period. This book in some ways could be seen to express something of the attempt by the youth to perform a redefinition of their country. On a social level, it sketches out some of what is and what is not accepted as appropriate behaviour in this formative modern society. In many cases what was formally taboo is now considered permissible.

The stories contain examples of the confusions, the presumed expectations, the habits, the sordid reality of life and the challenge to overcome it. They also reveal what activities these students and graduates partake in, what they discuss, with special focus on their entertainment practices.

I have included a quote from a famous Irish traditional song or poem before each story to give the reader a sense of the culture, wit and song which is ubiquitous in Irish life. The quotes are not intended to reference the stories although in some cases they do.

Although this is essentially a book of individual stories, they are drawn together by several common themes which will become apparent to the reader. They are linked also by the title, in that returning to the 'gaff' or place of residence forms an important part of the stories.

As I mentioned, there is the common background of the Celtic Tiger period in Ireland with daily life being expressed through the experiences of characters in their mid-twenties to early thirties. The characters are intended to symbolise some of the peculiarities and excesses of today's Ireland. Most are of eccentric and struggle with vice in some form or other such as sex, alcohol abuse, drugs or violence.

I saw no point in relaying the life of an ordinary resident who typically engages in the mundane and the predictable, instead the people who appear are creations that reflect the reality of life for Ireland's more outrageous citizens. The ordinary is not regarded with high esteem; important only is the realistic but extraordinary.

I have utilised what I call Marvellous Realism, a variety of literary realism where instead of the commonplace, the extraordinary is recounted. Instead of the dull incessant attention to detail, to comprehend the story, the reader is given sufficient information in the form of movement and action. In literary fiction, this realism can provide great insight and does not necessarily cause conflict with the feeling of escapism which is enjoyed during reading. Instead it runs parallel with this other necessary aspect of any good read.

The type of realism I envisage is an extraordinary variety, where non-ordinary reality blurs with fiction, becoming 'Marvellous Realism.'

During the editing of this collection, some people close to me highlighted the parallels with Joyce's *Dubliners*. These, for me, were unwanted and surprising. I had imagined that due to the lascivious nature of the pieces no parallel could exist.

I had consciously grouped together a series of narratives which examined and revealed the underbelly of modern Ireland, celebrating characters who ranged from desperate and misguided to highly irresponsible. These often self-destructive individuals are not glorified in our society but they embody the humanity of our experience.

But while Joyce's collection was inspiring, it did not form a direct inspiration. When revisiting his work years after the initial publication of this collection, I immediately became aware of some shared features. Both are collections of stories gathered under several definite themes. Both are mostly concentrated on Dublin, and feature many of Dublin's well-known pubs. Both include 15 stories, and are the first works of new writers. The final parallel was that while *Dubliners* was published in 1914, *Back to the Gaff* was first published exactly 100 years later in 2014. While writing and editing for the initial limited print run in 2014, for some reason I was completely unaware of some of these rather obvious parallels.

In the continuing effort to add meaning to Ireland's capital city and the country in general, it is important to look at the figures that have created our modern cultural interpretations of the city. Musicians, novelists and poets such as the following, some born in Dublin, some having moved there to ply their trade, have given such joy and identity to the Fair City though their successes.

Luke Kelly, with his distinguished ballad voice, Ronnie Drew with his sincere Dublin accent to the forefront in his singing, Pete St John who has written at least two of our most famous ballads, *Fields of Athenry* and *Dublin in the Rare Auld Times*, James Joyce who wrote the foremost novel in the English language, Patrick Kavanagh, who immortalised rural Ireland through his poetry about ordinary life, Brendan Behan, as famous for being a drinker as a playwright, poet, songwriter, republican and writer in both English and Irish Gaelic, George Bernard Shaw, playwright and Nobel Prize winner, Samuel Beckett, novelist, poet, playwright and winner of the Nobel Prize who wrote in both English and French, Seán O'Casey, celebrated for *Juno and the Paycock* and *The Plough and the Stars* among other great plays, Oscar Wilde, illustrious playwright who was involved in Decadent and Aesthetic movements, William Butler Yeats, highly-regarded poet and champion of the Irish Literary Revival, John Millington Synge, writer of *The Playboy of the Western World* and an important figure alongside Yeats in the Irish Literary Revival.

It is important also to recognise the role of the brave men and women who gave their lives for their country in the Easter Rising of 1916, making the ultimate sacrifice for their belief in freedom. Of these, the seven signatories of the Proclamation of the Irish Republic deserve particular attention: Pádraig Mac Piarais, James Connelly, Éamonn Ceannt, Thomas Clarke, Thomas MacDonagh, Seán MacDiarmada and Joseph Plunkett.

Their significance to modern Ireland cannot be underestimated and having celebrated the centenary of this major date in recent years, it helps us to remember the heroism and resolve shown by these and the many other men and women who took part. Michael Collins' name has not been afforded nearly the fame it deserves in this writers opinion, considering what he achieved in the aftermath of the revolution. Thanks to these people we have today's Republic of Ireland which is one of the safest, friendliest and most comfortable places to live anywhere in the world. I am proud to call myself an Irish citizen.

For all that is past and all that is to come, this is a documentation of the outrageous which is real and present, if at times partially obscured, in our contemporary society.

Have you ever been in love, me boys, Oh! have you felt the pain?
I'd sooner be in jail, myself, than be in love again.

From *The Garden Where the Praties Grow* (Johnny Patterson) as performed by John McCormack

Flash Dresser

Jen wasn't aware that 'Nike,' her live-in boyfriend of two years, was a lying, philandering, piece of garbage, at least not until she got a call from one of her girlfriends that morning.

He had been seen the night before in the arms of another, at McGowan's, a cheesy club that he always refused to bring her to. It was conclusive evidence, Jen thought to herself, because it came from Sherry, and she had always been a good friend, never a bitch. She had no reason to stir trouble and anyway the way she told it, it had sounded plausible.

He was bent over the bar drinking his usual Jack and Coke, with his arm around that slapper, a cheap tart from the north side. Since Jen left the north side she never discussed it, it was almost as if she had never been there, let alone lived there half her life.

The cheap tart had been whispering in his ear and pulling at his shirt, she probably brought home a new one every weekend, the tramp. Then when she brought him out on the dance floor he just stood there and did his one hand punch in the air, which was as close as he ever got to grooving.

The tart was rubbing herself all over him and then dragging him off the dance floor again, to make out with him on one of the sofas. She had danced for him like a stripper, maybe she was a stripper, maybe she had done lap dances before. Maybe she even... No. Jen couldn't think of it anymore.

They had left together. They probably had sex in the car. She had found that packet of condoms there that time. He said he'd forgotten to bring them in. She had believed him. Oh it was too much.

Jen drained her second glass of vodka and coke, although she'd had so little coke left that it was mostly vodka. Her head began to spin just a little, but she was fine, she told herself. That bastard! How could he go with someone else? And how come he picked such a tramp? That was the real insult. She was much better than that, her, Jen, she was a good woman, she told herself.

She went back into the kitchen and looked for the vodka. It was hidden at the back of the press, although when she had put it back there, she knew she'd be back to root it out soon after. She poured another double, or was it a triple, she didn't care. She even tried drinking some of it straight, to get a more immediate effect. It just made her wretch. She poured some coke on top, to at least give it a colour.

She thought of Nike, that bastard, how he used to stand looking at himself in *her* long mirror before going to the pub. *Her* mirror! Then obviously, he was going out and meeting tarts. She'd cut his balls off.

But wait, there were better things to do, things that would really annoy him. His friends called him 'Nike' because of his obsession with brand names. He bought new clothes every week. He was worse than her, but at least she needed new dresses to wear to all the weddings that were coming up this year. He just went to the pub, and then got off with slappers!

She began to cry. Her eyes had been holding it back for a while but now it was no use. She sat on the ground, with the big box of tissues beside her. 'Man-size' the box said. She'd make him cry alright.

She drank more. The glass was now almost empty but she was too upset to get up and refill it. The tears slowly subsided. He would pay! Him and all his flashy clothes! She staggered to her feet and crashed into the door on her way to the bedroom. That bastard! She opened the wardrobe and looked at all his branded shirts, fancy jeans that each cost twice what she paid for hers. Seven pairs of trainers, three of them never even worn, he would never get the chance!

She, in a fit of rage, threw his clothes on the ground and stamped on them. Then seeing all those smart shirts lying there, thought of him sucking up to slappers in them. She opened the window of their rented house which was just off the main road, and flung out a few shirts. That was better, she thought. Picking up trainers, she flung them out too. Then the jeans went. She even threw his pants out, the ones with the Pinocchio on the front. She used to think they were funny.

Just at that moment Joe the Junkie happened to be walking by. Joe was wondering where he'd get some gear; he hadn't had a hit since that morning. His head ached, his stomach groaned as he looked in car windows hoping someone might have left their bag or their wallet in view. All he had was a bit of hash he'd gotten down by the port but it had almost no effect anymore.

He stopped in his tracks when he saw a tennis shoe come flying onto the road in front of him. No one else seemed to notice. He picked it up and examining it, was sure it was new. If he just had the other one he might be able to sell them and get some cash. He then noticed the pile of clothes strewn across Jen's lawn. There were shirts, jeans – a whole wardrobe. It was junkie's Christmas!

Joe stole into the lawn, looking around him as he went and gathered as much stuff as he could carry. He picked up fancy T shirts, various odd shoes, maybe managing to get a matching pair, before leaving in a dash.

Upstairs Jen felt a bit sick. Her head was spinning again. She knew just before it came but it was too late. She vomited on the bedroom floor. Crawling towards the en suite bathroom she reached for the toilet bowl. She clung on to that bowl as the world spun around her. All she could do was hold on.

Nike had been working all day and when he parked his painter's van in front of the house, he was surprised to see several familiar looking garments lying on the lawn. In a state of distress, he got out and hurriedly began picking up his precious clothes. When he got inside he saw the vodka bottle, the vomit and Jen's face.

'You bastard,' she screamed and threw a clothes hanger at him.

'What d'ya think yer doing? Have you lost your mind?'

He placed his branded clothes on the

floor, shoes, jeans and soiled shirts. He investigated the wardrobe and found that more items were missing.

'What were ya doin' with me clothes?'

'You dirty cheating bastard!' she screamed.

So she knew. Now his fears were confirmed. It became apparent that half his clothes were missing but he couldn't talk to her about it now. It was better they stay away from each other for a while to calm down.

Nike quickly changed into whatever flashy clothes were left and made for the pub. He needed a drink. He was still hung-over and tired from last night's escapade. He had spent most of the day thinking about those breasts. Man they were great! But she was so stupid. He doubted he could endure her again tonight if she called.

He got to The International on Wicklow Street and had his usual few pints of lager before taking on the inevitable Jack and Coke. He needed to tell someone what had happened. Most of them knew about his deeds of the night before and had expected him to spend the night bragging.

Instead he had a drawn look on his face and began to relate an entirely different story.

'I was just pullin' in me van, right, and I saw all these clothes on the lawn. Shirts, jeans, the lot! I bloody flipped, man!'

Nike finished his pint and continued the story: 'My missus has lost it lads! I mean what ya doin' with my clothes like?'

As he was talking, in walked Joe the Junkie with a plastic bag in either hand.

'Alright lads?' said Joe walking up to one of Nike's friends. 'Would you be interested in some flash clothes?'

'Where'd you get'im?'

'I got nice shirts here, looka dat!' Joe the Junkie took out some expensive, slightly soiled shirts out of a bag. He then presented the lads with a pair of Nike's trainers.

'There're lovely, aren't they?'

Nike's eyes widened as blood ran to his muscles. He looked at the junkie and screamed.

'I am gonna break your fucking neck, you junkie bastard!' Nike got up from his barstool and grabbed Joe the Junkie by the throat.

'You robbed them from my place didn't you? You picked them up on my garden, you slimy bastard!'

Nike had plenty of support in the bar, but being big and angry he didn't need it. Joe the Junkie wasn't looking for a fight; he just wanted to get high. He watched fearfully as Nike straightened up to hit him. He gave it up.

'Ok, alright, I took them from a garden. I didn't know who owned them...they were just thrown out, like.'

Nike took a closer look at the junkie. Not only was he trying to sell Nike's clothes, he was also decked out head to toe in them.

'Right you know what you're gonna do? You're gonna strip! Right here, right now, you cheeky fecker.'

'What? Here in the pub?' pleaded Joe. Nike clenched his fist and raised it slowly.

In fear of his life, Joe the Junkie took off the stolen jeans, runners, hoodie and t-shirt while the whole pub looked on, mouths open. Joe was down to his underpants. 'They're mine,' he protested.

Nike's mates were in raptures.

'Get them off ya!' said one. Nike considered it but decided to let him go at that.

Joe the Junkie retrieved the belt, claiming it was his.

'Put it on then!' said Nike.

Joe the Junkie stood in the bar, still in fear of his life and put the belt on around his boxers.

'Now get the hell outta here,' shouted Nike, 'and don't rob anymore from me!'

Joe the Junkie stepped out into the cold November air in just his underpants. Another junkie passed and was surprised to see Joe in such attire.

'Joe, why are you wearing a belt around your boxers?'

Joe the Junkie shivered and looking at the ground, he mumbled, 'It's a long story.'

[Accepted for publication at Roadside Fiction]
http://roadsidefiction.com/

You may take the shamrock from your hat
And cast it on the sod,
But 'twill take root and flourish still
Tho' underfoot 'tis trod.

From *The Wearing of the Green* (Dion Boucicault)
as performed by John McCormack

Classic Tractor

As I approached the counter I realised that I was interrupting his reading. He finally gazed up at me from behind a copy of *Classic Tractor*.

'Serious weather,' I commented socially. He seemed unaware of the existence of anything outside of the room.

'D'ya have much work on d'day?' I enquired.

'Not a hate, no. I was thinking I might go on the beer,' he replied putting down the magazine. I thought he would too; Tom usually had a thirst on him.

'Did ya get the silage done?' he asked.

'I did,' I replied picking up his magazine and looking at the picture of the John Deere on the front. John Deere was the Ferrari of the tractor world (or should that be the 'pin-up?'). The beauty was not lost on Tom.

'Has Gerry much on d'day?' Gerry was his neighbour and never had anything on, except during the summer, when he would cut every blade of grass in the area. He would typically arrive at an undisclosed hour with his tractor, an International 4-wheel drive, animal of a machine, with a rotary mower attached.

He was so in demand this time of year that he usually avoided answering his mobile phone. If you were lucky and got him, or luckier still, he called you the call would usually have the drone of the big tractor in full rev in the background. He was a contractor or a cowboy or maybe both. He was known to fall out with

10

those in his employment as well as the farmers that employed him. He did not discriminate - he hated everybody.

'Gerry is on the go a lot; well he's kept going anyways.' I got the feeling that Tom wanted to slip back into the world of *'Classic Tractor'* so I came to the point.

'D'ya think you'll see him later?' It was a long shot. Tom might not even be able to see his pint of stout later.

'I haven't spoken to that man in weeks,' he said. I was surprised. Something was up, they were usually constant buddies. Gerry had been over at Tom's house nearly every evening for months.

'I'll tell him you were askin' for him,' said Tom reaching for the magazine again.

'Will ya? Good man, I have just the wee bit at the back of the house to cut and bale.'

'Will ya be makin' more silage?'

'No, I'll do hay. I usually make the few bales for the horses you know, they like the bit of hay.'

'Right-o,' said Tom growing impatient. I reached around and picked up a bag of two-inch nails just not to leave without buying something. He might be talking about me otherwise.

Two days later Gerry finally called me. It seems that he did so as a result of my relentless pestering of him by phone rather than having received Tom's message.

*

Gerry stood looking at the field of grass. He gave it a long look and then announced he'd have to charge a bit extra for the work this year because he had a few problems with the bailer.

'Sure, that comes with the job,' I informed him, and he should be expecting that things would break and need to be fixed. 'That's part of your overheads,' I mentioned with authority. Gerry was not of the same mind-set.

'Listen here!' he demanded, holding out his hand which gradually was becoming a fist, 'Don't you dictate to me!' He took a step closer invading my space.

'I know my overheads, so I do. You don't know what it costs to run this thing,' he said it as he patted the tractor on the front wheel with careful devotion. 'Don't you be tellin' me what it costs.'

He was clearly keen to get back into the tractor and start mowing. Conversation was something he did only with a few pints in him and even then it could be erratic. It would have been more profitable to converse with his beloved tractor than he who was riled so easily.

'Well, I'll let you get on with it,' I said having had about enough of his ignorance. He spat on the ground and then got into his tractor. He would not put much love into the job now, I thought.

*

Gerry had finished up for the season and was to be found night after night in the foulest smelling of the local bars. He sat at the end of the counter by a wall where he could avoid needless conversation. The pints of stout were going down well, he thought as he looked at the small amount that remained in his glass.

'Jimmy put on another one there, will

ya?'

'Right you be, Gerry!' said Jimmy the barman as he picked up a dirty glass and began to pour. Jimmy thought that an effective method of cleaning glasses was rinsing them under the tap for a few seconds. The night was over for most punters as they first put on their jackets and then drained the last out of their glasses. Only 4 drinkers remained. Closing time was two hours ago but this meant nothing to Jimmy the unwashed and un-washing barman. The phone rang. Jimmy picked it up and answered, 'Well!' Someone on the other end of the line wanted to know if he was still open. It was a precarious question depending on who was asking. Jimmy, however, recognised the voice.

'Ah is that you Tom?'

'Yeah. Would we be fit ta get a pint with ya?'

'Well, where are ya now?'

'Up the road at O'Neills. They're all done here. We'll be down to ya in two minutes. Is that alright?'

'Ah right Tom, just give a wee knock on the window. But just to tell ya, Gerry is in here,' advised Jimmy.

'Ach, sure me and Gerry's the best a friends!' Tom informed.

'Alright see ya in a minute.'

Jimmy dropped the phone and strolled over to Gerry.

'Listen! Tom McGivney is on his way in here now, just to let ya know like.'

Gerry wasn't going to be moved by no

man and simply responded. 'Sure, what's that to me?'

The last time Gerry and Tom had the pleasure of meeting, Gerry had thrown a hammer at him. The time before that was worse. Jimmy the barman was doing the decent thing by putting Gerry in the picture.

Gerry picked up his pint, drained it and ordered another. He thought about his last encounter with Tom. He had been driving down the road when he saw Tom standing outside his house working on his fence. Gerry stopped to give out to him about money that he still owed for work done the year before.

'Any sign of ya payin' me for that bit a work, for the love of Jesus?' Gerry asked out of the driver's window.

'Sure, I told ya I'd give it to ya when I'm good and ready!' said Tom defiantly.

He got out of his jeep and walked up to him. 'But sure, it was done last year. What are ya playin' at?'

'Listen here you, get back into that jeep and get off down the road with ya,' said Tom.

Gerry looked at him squarely. 'I'm not goin' nowhere till ya tell me you're gonna pay me.'

'Go away ya hoor ya!' said Tom without sweetness.

Gerry swung for his left jaw. Tom caught a clean box in the face. He immediately swung back but Gerry was tough and too hard to hit. Gerry hit him again, this time in the nose. Tom's nose exploded. Little rivers of bright red blood cascaded down onto his lips and chin.

Tom drove forward and clattered into Gerry sending him backwards. Tom swung and missed again. Gerry was off balance trying to avoid the blow. Tom went forward, blood dripping off his chin. He shoved Gerry towards the briars. Gerry lost his footing and went tumbling into the ditch. He was enveloped in a labyrinth of briars and nettles. He could feel thorns and stings on his hands. There was a small stream of water running underneath and this soaked his rear end. Tom backed off laughing loudly.

'Now look at you, ya auld bollox.'

Gerry struggled for a few minutes to untangle himself from the mess of briars and bushes that held him. He got up finally and stepped out onto the road, his ass soggy and his pride drenched. Tom stood a distance away by his house laughing at the poor creature.

Gerry had passed by in his jeep again a few days later and seeing Tom out in front of his house he got ready. He gripped a hammer from his toolbox and rolled down the window. Gerry slowed down as he neared but Tom spotted him coming. Tom's eyes opened wide, expecting trouble. Gerry let swing with the hammer aiming for Tom's head. Tom ducked and it flew by him. Gerry put the foot down and drove on.

That was a few weeks ago. Presently he sat in the bar awaiting Tom's entrance. He sipped quietly at his pint. The secret knock came at the window and Jimmy the barman scurried out obediently to open up. Tom and two others arrived in, well oiled.

'Well Gerry!' Tom shouted over when he saw him. Gerry didn't like the tone of it. He looked over at Tom for a second and back at his pint. Tom and his cronies sat down and drank.

Half an hour later Gerry got up and made for the toilet. Tom waited a few seconds and then followed him. It transpired that Gerry was in bad shape, even worse shape than Tom. He struggled to walk with any elegance.

Tom opened the toilet door and watched as Gerry gave it a shake and put it away. Then he swung. A helpless Gerry, little more than a sitting duck, took one to the cheek, then another to the chin. He fell back against the urinals. His ass was soaked again only this time it was notably worse.

His pride took another one in the nose. Gerry, however, tough as an old boot, managed to stumble forward and clock Tom one in the nose. Tom's nose opened again. He could feel the blood reach his chin. He lost the appetite for violence and returned to the bar.

'Have you an auld bit of a tissue there Jimmy?'

Gerry struggled out of the toilets head spinning, ass soaked. He waddled onwards past Tom and out of the bar. Tom roared at him. 'Ya auld bollox!'

Tom's cronies looked at the mess that was Tom's nose. 'Why didn't you pay Gerry in the first place and avoid all this trouble?' they wanted to ask. Instead they humoured him saying, 'You gave him a hell of a doin'! He won't be throwing any more hammers at ya now! Are ya havin' a pint?'

Back to the Gaff

[Originally published at Zouchmagazine.com on 22/1/2014]
http://zouchmagazine.com/classic-tractor/

Down by the salley gardens my love and I did meet;
She passed the salley gardens with little snow-white feet.
She bid me take love easy, as the leaves grow on the tree;
But I, being young and foolish, with her would not agree.

From *Down by the Salley Gardens* (W.B Yeats) as performed by John McCormack

The Duke

Dublin, 2006

I met a girl in a bar the usual way, whatever the hell that is, a few days before and we had exchanged numbers. I waited the normal amount of time before contacting her, so as not to frighten her off or give her the impression that I was over-interested. While I was waiting she contacted me.

Next came the complicated procedure of choosing a place to meet. I had to choose a place where I would feel comfortable, where the music was loud, but not too loud, where the lights were low, but not too low, where there were people, but not too many, the kind of place that indicates to her the kind of cool relaxed life I led, the kind of place that relations with said woman could flourish naturally, but most importantly the kind of place where the Guinness was good.

I invited her for a drink at Bruxelles, 'Dublin's Cosmopolitan Bar,' a place I frequented on occasion. We were to meet the following night. She agreed to meet me there but, in her calculated approach to the event, threw in a not so subtle hint that I had chosen a poor location.

Catherine: Oh aye so meet you there; might pick another location after a while though.

So rather than just meet me at the place

20

we had arranged, she being a strange sort of a woman, the kind that are usually most interesting, in fact, decided to get *scuttered* drunk with her friends at exactly the same time in a completely different location.

So, I threw a dinner into me, got ready to leave the house to meet her at the time and place agreed. I then received a text message from the strange woman on that often socially retarded piece of equipment they call a mobile phone. The message was simple: She was waiting for me at The Duke. I began to write a reply but immediately the phone rang.

'Hey! Are you coming in? When do you think you'll be here?' she said all at once.

There was no more or no less to it, if I expected an explanation I wasn't getting it. I simply had to appear there. I prepared to go into town via Dublin's wonderfully confused bus service.

'It's the worst public transport system in the EU,' I heard a young guy at the bus stop remark in a Sunny South-East accent. 'They're all feckin' eejits. I've been here half a feckin' hour man!' He looked at me expectantly. Would I agree with this stranger simply to appease him?

Now it wouldn't be my style to passionately defend the merits of Dublin Bus but nonetheless, I asked him: 'Where else in the EU have you been?' What had he to compare it to, I wondered.

It transpired that this opinionated country blow-in had been to Germany once.

'Where else?' I waited.

'What do you mean?' he demanded. He looked at me confused, as though with this, he had already established proof that he was a cosmopolitan gent, free from prejudice and suitably qualified by experience to make this statement. I pointed out that Germany was only one country and that a visit there did not represent a comprehensive understanding of European Union inner city transport services.

I was about to inform him that Germany had one of the most efficient transport networks if not in the world, then certainly in Europe since post World War II redevelopments and that comparing Dublin's transport services to those of the biggest economy in Europe was unrealistic but then the bus came. I had been waiting 5 minutes. Most of that time had flown by anyway putting this fiend in his place.

I walked up Grafton Street, taking a left onto Duke Street passing a busker who sang *Dirty Old Town* with solemn conviction. When I got to the door of the bar it struck me - What the hell did she look like?

As most blossoming relationships in Dublin have their roots in a night under the heavy sedation of 'a drop of the hard stuff,' I was suitably confused as to her appearance. Was she tall? Yes, well tall'ish. Slim? Yes. Was she good looking? I think so (I had been lucky) well I wasn't really sure but I guessed I would soon find out...

The bar was very busy and filled by loud conversation, fanatical laughter and the smell of stout. I went inside and trying to take everything and everyone in, staring wildly around me I almost forgot to look where I was going. I immediately bumped into her. She looked just as surprised as I was.

She led me upstairs to a where her friends were and unknown territory. I was presented to a table of wide-eyed strangers all of whom knew the circumstances of my arrival. She worked with these introverted strangers in a busy book shop, she told me later. They were mostly passably attractive, intelligent females ranging from early to late twenties. Bumbling introductions followed and then a long silence as some continued to gaze at me while others had seen enough to make up their minds. This moment was broken only by some hushed tones and whispers between some concerning her selection of date material.

She saw that I was now sitting alone, not talking to anyone, so she charitably sat down beside me. At this point I will finally name her. She is Catherine, a Dubliner, a hippy and a ball of energy.

'I've just had 6 pints,' she slurred merrily. I was astounded. I was not surprised at an Irish girl drinking so much or that this was her preparation for meeting a new date. No. I was shocked because she held it so well. Not a sign of drunkenness about her. Next she confessed to being awake for 36 hours straight:

'I didn't get to bed last night,' she remarked and began to tell a story of suitable madness which passed over my head the way clouds do.

'I need a cigarette,' she said quickly. 'Do you smoke?'

'Yeah, why not?' I replied so that I could get outside with her away from the staring faces.

'Well, let's go out for a fag,' she asserted and we left the table, her leading the way, marching confidently towards the exit. Everyone was looking for their coats and it seemed as though we would soon be alone at the table anyway. There was much confusion as ten drunken girls searched for their jackets. It appeared as though they would have left the bar before we returned.

Outside Catherine talked at the pace of something really fast.

'I've got these friends,' she excitedly revealed between puffs of her cigarette, 'and they're really cool, you'll like them.' I hated them already.

'They live really close and they have loads of drugs. You like weed? Everybody does.'

Her chat was like Speedy Gonzales after a simultaneous mainline of amphetamine and cocaine. Not waiting for me to express any interest in this proposition, she continued to sell this idea to me pointing out that she wasn't going to any more bars. She added that if I didn't want to go I could go to Monkeyland or wherever I wanted, because she would be going anyway.

It transpired that she had already arranged to call over to their house. This was on top of arranging to meet the group of wide-eyed, book loving, work colleagues upstairs in The Duke, yours truly for our supposed 'date,' which was supposed to be in a different bar.

There was no debate. We left and began

walking to the house of ill repute which it became apparent, was not really close at all. Fascination was the only explanation for my sustained presence, as her outlandish and recklessly exciting life intrigued me. It was certainly better than sitting in my cold kitchen, drinking tea and wondering when I'd meet an interesting female.

We walked and walked and she opened her ears for the first time to put me on the spot. She quizzed me on my interests, ambitions, musical taste (which was of critical importance apparently) and my general habits as a human being. She was a woman after all, and I had now discovered she was maybe not so strange.

We hit it off to a great extent on our walk through the south inner city. As Renelagh got closer and my feet wearied she finally announced: 'We're there.'

She addressed the intercom of a flat in an old historic Georgian building. A female voice answered in audibly excited tones. A tall, bored looking, guy opened the door and barely managed to grumble a 'hello.'

Not good, I thought. I have to enter this stranger's dwelling and he appears to offer little in the way of welcome. Michael was his name and I think we would have gotten no further than that if not for the magic created by Catherine's colourful conversational techniques and general excitability.

Catherine ran up the stairs and greeted her good-looking friend. I remembered her face and unusually, her name also. It was Aoife, she had been at the bar when I met Catherine a few days previously. In fact my friend, also called Michael, had wasted an entire night trying to convince her they should be together in a strictly non-platonic capacity. She waited until the end of the night before telling him she already had a Michael and she was quite happy with him.

In their one room combined kitchen, living room, laundry room and music studio, I sat on an armchair and watched Catherine and Aoife relentlessly embrace and laugh. They loved each other - it was obvious.

Michael sat across from me on a sofa, looking now slightly more bored. He had assembled the necessary items to construct a joint. While this industrious young man busied himself at what he considered to be the first point of hospitality, I asked him about his large collection of musical equipment. He answered cryptically and as briefly as possible.

He had a huge Mac which continually displayed rotations of album covers from his collection. In the absence of conversation this occupied my attention. Next to this was a keyboard, various pedals and boxes which were all connected by a myriad of cables.

Soon we were getting baked in the hot Dublin night. Twenty minutes or so must have elapsed since we arrived at the house and by now time and space was becoming something transient and detached. It was then that I began to notice some changes in the girls. They had moved from the sofa and armchair respectfully and were now in the throes of a merry dance around the kitchen. Another unusual thing occurred: they offered me pills. (E, Ex, yokes, ecstasy).

'Let's take some pills!' Catherine suggested with eager impatience.

'Come on Michael you'll take one!' they urged the piece of stone sitting across from me.

'No I'm tired,' he responded in the monotone sound he preferred to speech. They didn't let up there.

'Go on!' they shouted.

'No, I'm too tired, gonna go to sleep soon,' he tried, pleaded almost.

'Ah, sure it'll wake ya up a bit!' Catherine persisted, sensing weakness. Maybe he was about to give in. They continued to press him and at last he agreed. He consumed it swiftly and thoughtlessly in a manner befitting one accustomed to such things.

I had no interest in taking Class A drugs with people I didn't know, in a place I was not familiar with, late at night and miles from home. Also the prospect of talking to a human stone while higher than the Sears Tower appealed to me not at all.

Michael and Aoife looked at each other for perhaps the first time all night (she had been distracted by Catherine's arrival and besides, as I mentioned earlier, he was quite boring) although they were going out together and sharing the same house.

'I just moved in last week,' Aoife had informed me. They began to share a private moment which allowed my 'date' and I to do likewise.

'You want to take one?' she persisted, concentrating on me.

'No, it's not my thing,' I said for hopefully, the last time.

'Ok, well do mind if I take one?' She looked me in the eye.

'You can do whatever you want,' I said hoping she would choose not to.

'Well, I actually already did!' she confessed, 'I dropped it when we got to the house. So did Aoife. And they're starting to kick in!' she announced. She looked fixedly at me then broke into little distracted smiles before looking back again. The drug was working on her.

'You don't mind do you?' she asked for my approval again.

'No, it's cool,' I assured her, although I considered that the situation dramatically differed from 'cool.'

I sat back on the armchair as I watched the surreal sight before me. The two girls were dancing around the kitchen to some horrific blend of traffic noise, hooting, shouting, pumping shite they considered a suitable musical choice.

I looked over at the stone. He was in the latter stages of constructing another mind bending smoking mixture.

I sat for a few minutes taking it all in. The sounds of laughter and intoxication from the girls were louder now. They danced on the spot in the kitchen, eyes locked on each other and smiling from ear to ear.

'Wow it's great!' said one, shaking her head around.

I looked back at the conversational

cabbage on the sofa who was now virtually in a coma while still possibly awake. I think he called it living.

The girls turned their attention to us, coming over and dancing relentlessly in front of the sofa. They were looking for some gesture of reassurance. They rolled around on the ground, talked rubbish, laughed and then danced again. This was amusing for the first hour or so then I had enough. They seemed to be locked on repeat.

Time to get out of here. I got up and made like I was going to leave. Catherine protested, insisting I should take a pill and join them dancing or at least hang around until later. She gave me a suggestive wink to make sure I got the message. I was leaving and that was it. She went into a sudden guilty terror.

'Oh no! I ignored you all night and now you're gonna leave and not call me again.'

She hugged me and I tried to dislodge myself, assuring her that I would indeed call and meet her again soon.

She kissed me, pressing her breasts into my chest. I could have stayed but I didn't.

[Originally published on Hackwriters.com 31/1/2014]
http://www.hackwriters.com/DukeJPB.htm

I wish them both much joy though they can't hear me
And may God reward him well for the slighting of me.

From *The Blacksmith* (Traditional) as performed by Andy Irvine and Planxty

The Duke Part II

Catherine was magnetic. It had all started in a dark, crowded room and I had decided to risk finding out where it might lead.

When we met on subsequent occasions, as luck would have it, she wasn't off her head on pills and we talked freely. Freely became excitedly and I was compelled to invite her back to the gaff. I ended up seeing her several times that week.

Our bodies were compelled to touch at every moment. Standing near other we either hugged roughly or held hands and danced to the unheard music of new romance. We took wild salsa-style dances through the grey streets of Cabra on the way to childishly discover mischief.

Her first message after our bizarre date night arrived with similar strangeness.

Catherine: Forces of darkness
              must be held at bay.
              Are you still on for the
              party tonight?
              Catherine with a C.

Well what else am I doing? Of course I'd meet her. I couldn't even remember what party she had been on about but it mattered not. Some more odd messages followed until she sent this:

Catherine: Ahem how sorry, I was
              just being sarcastic in

32

the text yesterday I
actually am interested
in meeting you. I didn't
take pills last night so
feeling good.

Well, how can you refuse such a frank statement? The tone employed suggested that I had caught her on one of only a few good days.

That night we met and spent the whole evening wired in each other's presence, jabbering endlessly. I was pedestrian compared to her. Her will to live was astounding. I could never predict her next move or what adventure we might embark on. We might go to meet some of the many odd people she knew, randomly get drunk together, make out at my house; explore deserted parts of the city; it was never certain.

Becoming interested in her, I sent a message asking how her night out went and if she wanted to do something the next day. She texted me back a day late:

Catherine: Yo a night of unforeseen
wonders it was. Went
to a playground at
10am. Phone was dead
till now. Sure where
and when? Hope you
got all that some people
don't.

She wanted to meet on Tuesday night but I was too stuck in my ways and absorbed in my working week. I also got the feeling she'd meet me whenever I decided so out of cruel selfishness I put her off till Wednesday saying I had something to do.

Catherine: It's more like a minor catastrophe really. Why can't you? Don't know if Wednesday is ok French friend leaving do, pity as had wed off.

She agreed as I thought she might. I was beginning to take her for granted and she knew it.

Catherine: Compromise I can't and I won't. Different bat time same bat place?

We met in town and had a gorgeous pint in the Stag's Head but soon the need to roll around in bed came to the surface. A few days of Catherine at my house followed. In fact I wondered if she would ever leave. Her mother rang at one point to ask where she was.

'I haven't seen you in three days. Where are you?'

'It's all good, Mum. Don't worry I'll be home before you know it!'

Heavy mum-speak followed which she listened to with obligatory patience.

'Ok Mum, I gotta go now...I'll see you soon, OK? Bye.'

*

After our intense three days together I

was enjoying some quiet time. She got in touch again:

Catherine: Yo is my sisters scarfy thing that I drape fashionably on my head in your house? Please tell me it is so.

I had it and told her I would keep it for her. I asked if she was at home, expecting after her long stay at mine that she might need to wash some clothes and chill out a bit.

Catherine: Nein I ist in Aoife and Martin's having a smoke and getting fed which is what somebody I'll not mention names here forgot to do earlier.

She lambasted me for not feeding her even though she had passed up every offer of food that I sent her way. There was no winning that argument. She waited till the following day to answer my rebuke. She, of course, wanted to meet again.

Catherine: Bucko I chose not to dignify your text with an answer. Any self-respecting humanitarian would have known that a bowl of chicken broth was in order. Are you out?

I made a reference to the variety of folk that would be out on a Monday night: lunatics, alcoholics and the odd sane person.

Catherine: Yeah Jimbo and you wouldn't be one of them. Nothing much in town. When am I getting my scarf back? When is the next full moon?

Rather than go into town and feck around, lazily I decided to ask her to come over. I was doing myself out of a good experience by not following her wild unpredictability. I knew it but I had no will to chase her around.

Catherine: Bud are you talking about me coming over tonight? I may do what Nightlink goes out to yours?

That night I had been sitting with my new flatmates and their friends drinking beer and was not about to go anywhere. Luckily she was transport friendly. When she arrived I had to introduce her to the large group. She was nervous so we just shied away onto a sofa, letting them talk amongst themselves. Despite her infectious personality, she was not a wilful purveyor of new social stratospheres.

Back to the Gaff

A few days later and feeling at the peak of laziness I asked her to come round again. She had left her phone at Aoife and Martin's place, the obvious next stop after leaving my abode it seemed. When she went home I couldn't imagine. She offered feeble protest but would ultimately come round.

> Catherine: Hey, hey, hey, got my phone back. Why do I need to go to your house? What are the buses again?

The following week I found out she had made plans to go drinking and fecking around in Cork. A noble pursuit no doubt. She would be there over the weekend so she wanted to meet mid-week. I was up to other things though and was reeling a little, overwhelmed by her intense company. Had I the will to lift myself out of the pit I was falling into, I would have gone with her.

> Catherine: To dip in the shallows of infinity indeed would be a fine thing. At the '40 Foot.' Was out grave hopping. I'm heading down on Friday. Do you want to meet up?

> Catherine: Alree man see you after Cork. Enjoy yourself! x

We kept in touch while she was down there. I had to keep the lines of communication open especially in light of the fact that I had let her down by not wanting to meet before she left. She had grown attached to one of my hoodies which fitted better and looked better on her than me. I silently conceded it to her since she wore it constantly, during all daytime hours. 'Any insanity in Cork?' I had asked.

Catherine: Ya bleedin wimp. A heap of neuroses but no insanity as of yet but hey the night is young. Your top has seen some sweaty mingholes though.

I'd been devouring whatever Bob Dylan material I could find at home while getting through a nice chunk of polm. I had to come up with something weird to compete with her consistently 'out there' messages. I decided on a song from *Highway 61 Revisited* which contained a peculiar reference to cows and giving people milk.

Catherine: Hey snuggums what song was that a quote from? Are you gigging tonight?

Message: *'Ballad of a Thin Man'* and don't call me stupid names.

Catherine: Sho ya donkey am I not allowed to use terms of affection well fine then! Watching match in Doyles do you wanna come along or meet up later?

I loved the 'Big D' or 'Doyles' to people outside the circle. I went in to meet her Sunday afternoon and watch some World Cup soccer which I had developed a passing interest in.

While there, the barman informed all and sundry of a prize draw which they were having after the game. It served to keep the drinkers in the pub. Some of Catherine's friends left and in a decent gesture, handed over their tickets for the draw. For the first time in my life, I won something that day – a bottle of vodka. It was a turning point of sorts.

She stayed with me that night and we lay close. I could feel her emotions become stronger. It happened suddenly in the end, but now that it was established there was no going back to the way it was before, at least not for her. The next day she left for wherever she went when she wasn't here. The day after she wanted to meet again.

Catherine: Pumpkinpoo how are you? Finished work at 7. Do you wish to meet up then or later? Hope you enjoyed playing with the candle wax

What the feck was she talking about? She was definitely touched. I asked her over, as I usually did. She would come, as she usually did.

Catherine: But of course sugar lump I will. What time shall we rendezvous?

Catherine: It will involve stealing some sort of transportational device and mad dash caper involving high speed car chases across town but be there I will.

We spent a few more days together at my house. During this time I got a call from a few friends who were hanging out at another house nearby. They wanted me to come over probably because they knew I had been off the radar for a few weeks and they suspected that a woman was involved.

'Hey John, are you coming over to Joe's house? There's a wild crew of us here and carnage is guaranteed!'

'Ah man I don't know if I'm gonna make it tonight...I'm a bit busy you know...'

'You're busy! Don't give me that shite! What are you doing?'

'Ah ... I'm courting!'

The voice on the other end of the line went into raptures of laughter.

'Courting?! I'm sure you mean you're engaging in some gnarly variety of casual sex!'

I couldn't keep the laughter in now either. Catherine looked curious. Then a girl came on the line.

'John, why won't you come over? And you know I'm leaving soon!'

I recognised the voice. She was one of those flirty girls that wanted all your time and never had any intention of doing anything. To hell with her and all her kind I said to myself.

'I can't tonight, I'm busy...'

'Look! I know you're naked in your bed with some girl and don't try to tell me it's not true!'

She was crying on the phone. I never thought she cared. Maybe she was just drunk.

'Come on! Look, I can't come round tonight but I'll see you soon ok?'

'You can go if you want,' said Catherine in the background. I definitely wasn't going after hearing how drunk and emotional the girl was. I'd be steering well clear.

Next morning before Catherine complained of not being fed I proceeded to fry some eggs. There was difficulty in getting them into the pan however. They either went in half beaten or with annoying pieces of shell complicating things by their presence.

Catherine regarded my failure and made her most memorable observation:

'Men can't crack eggs!'

It was true. No one had ever said it before but it couldn't be denied.

A few days later she texted me asking

for the number of a dope dealer for some guy she kind of knew. I hadn't one and even if I had I wouldn't be passing it out to people that I didn't know.

> Catherine: Indeedilidoodili it's not for him it's for John number is ----- what are you up to tomorrow?

I agreed to meet her the next day but made no definite arrangements on time. That evening Peter rang. I hadn't seen much of him since the charade with Catherine began. He wanted to go to the 'Big D.' I agreed to meet him at Doyle's knowing that meant a heavy night of carnage in the form of Guinness, moshing and coming home about 4am.

I hadn't gotten drunk with him in a while and so we launched into it spectacularly. A few well-mannered pints in the historic Palace Bar on Fleet Street led us conveniently towards a few messy ones in Doyle's.

Sometime in the night before I lost all sensory control, I noticed a stunning blonde dancing in front of me. I took two steps forward; that's all it took. She reeled around partially to have a look at me. I smiled and moved in. We began to kiss. Peter started laughing as he usually did when I began this kind of caper.

The girl in question was a Swede who had fallen in love with Dublin so much so that she decided to move there. I ran my fingers through her delicate blonde hair. I was smitten.

Half an hour of making out went by like one of those sweet dreams of the early morning. I got her number and was fairly sure she'd come through on meeting up.

'She's a cutie,' said Peter as we staggered off in the vague direction of home. 'You gonna see her again?'

'I have her number.'

'Hold onto her man, she's a good one!' he said quite seriously, dispensing friendly advice and pointing out what I had already decided on.

Next day I was lazing on the couch revisiting the night before. I was at that blissful point where all I could think of was how lucky I had been and how I was looking forward to seeing this new girl again.

My peace was shattered when the phone buzzed. It was Catherine. The guilt began to set in. The memory was still fresh from the previous night and I didn't want to erase it just yet. It was already ruined. I read the message.

Catherine: Listen you had better have broken all your fingers or else I'll break them for you. Some people would consider it polite to answer a text especially in light of the fact we were meant to meet up. My sympathies if you are lying in a coma.

There was nothing to say to such a message so I waited, gathering my thoughts. I wasn't going to meet her. It would be too strange in my present condition. Another message arrived an hour later.

Catherine: Well that was a really courageous way of breaking up with me...

Bemused, I reread the message a few times. Should I let her go? She was already gone. She probably wondered what had gone wrong. She probably went to Aoife and Martin's house to ask advice and to seek condolence. She had needed to vent some anger too, that was certain. She probably asked herself how it could have gone all wrong in such a short time. She probably wondered.

In the meantime I met the Swede for a few drinks and we made out. Two drinks arrived at our table and we looked around surprised. Two guys sitting at the next table had bought us a round of drink for no apparent reason.

'You two looked really in love,' said one of them finally. 'Don't buy me a drink back, just do it for someone else sometime.'

It was a noble gesture. We, of course, had to talk to them at length afterwards interrupting our soirée. It was our one and only as it turned out. She worked until 2am six nights a week so I'd never see her. She wished me all the best and told me to enjoy Dublin.

I had been doing just that up until this point. The wheels came off my fun. That was the end of it. There is, in fact, a moral of sorts to the story, something a wise old country woman told me once:

'If you try to sit on two stools, you end up on the floor.'

Thit muid i dtuirse 's i mbrón
Is d'fhiafraigh den óigbhean chaoin
'Cá bhfuigheas muid gloine le h-ól
A thógfadh an brón dar gcroí?'

From *Chuaigh mé 'na Rossann* (Traditional) as
performed by Clannad

Translation:
We fell into tiredness and sadness
And I asked the gentle young woman
'Where will we get a glass to drink
That would lift the sadness from our hearts?'

The Sport of Kings?

Rory sat in work looking at the clock. The 5:30 at Punchestown was about to start and a sole punter came running up to the counter with a last minute docket. Rory took the bet which distracted momentarily from his forlorn deliberations as to why he was in this dead end job. Soon the racing would be finished and he could close the shop and go for a pint. He was off the next day.

At 6pm, he met Michael his constant friend since the days of secondary school in rural County Cavan, and they set off for Mulligan's, Poolbeg Street. Both now worked for the same bookmaker in Dublin and frustrated with their positions, often exchanged tales of work-related woe.

Michael, the more reckless yet efficient of the two, had to be in work the next morning at ten, but as he was in the enviable position of living on the same street that he worked, he could stumble out of bed and make it in unshaven and generally unkempt. The bookie opened its doors around ten thirty but later if Michael slept in, which he was fond of doing especially after a few pints of stout.

On their night out the lads had consumed a generous supply of crude oil stout and soon hunger knocked on the door. They returned to Michael's house around 3 am armed with burgers and over-salted chips. Rory lived "out in the sticks" of Terenure and so avoided paying for a taxi home by electing for the convenience of Michael's couch.

Michael's new "gaff" was less than ideal from a point of view of comfort. There was no kitchen table and an old haggard stool served as a make shift, yet practical, communal dining-table. They brought the chips and burgers to Michael's room.

Rory groaned and complaining of his feet took off his shoes before devouring the fast food. Michael ate quickly and afterwards feeling suddenly tired, began to doze off. Rory bid him goodnight and headed for the splendour of the sitting room sofa where he lay trying to digest the indigestible.

Next morning Michael crawled out of bed and got together what he needed for work. He checked the time, locked his door and then made for work.

Mornings in the betting shop were slack in the extreme; all there was to do was tear out specific sections of the daily newspapers and attach them roughly to the boards around the shop. A feeble hung-over mind could accomplish this task most of the time.

The early prices for feature races would need to be written clearly on the whiteboard behind the counter. These odds could be scrawled in a vaguely horizontal manner or sketched in an artistic fashion, using imaginative colours, to attract often easily impressed punters to part with their cash. As for a regular punter, today is always your lucky day.

During the main part of the day, he sat at the counter for seemingly endless hours taking bets and watching punters approach the counter with the constancy of running water. They appeared to resemble zombies by the end of a long day.

Later in the day and long after Michael had left for work, Rory woke up on the sofa feeling less than bright-eyed. He began to prepare himself mentally for leaving the house out into the unknown wonders of Pearse Street.

He got up and investigated the disappearance of his shoes, then remembered that he had left them in Michael's room. He went to get them only to find that Michael had locked his bedroom door. He shouted at the door in anger as he remembered Michael telling him that he always kept it locked because of the devious housemate who potentially couldn't be trusted.

'What the hell was he going to do now?' he wondered. Everyone else had gone to work and he was alone in Michael's house in his bare feet. He grabbed his mobile phone and called Michael.

'Good day to you!' answered a cheerful Michael, 'How are you fixed?'

'Ah, not too good buddy. A man's mind could be broken and desperate,' a strained voice replied.

'Ha ha! That burger didn't dry up the stout then?' asked Michael.

An old man approached the counter and placed a docket before Michael with grubby brown tobacco-stained fingers. 'I'll take 16/1 on that,' he declared confidently.

'No. You can have 12/1.'

'Go 'way outta dat!' said the old Dubliner, 'I want 16/1'.

'It's gone into twelve to one now from sixteen's earlier.....what?....no, you can't have sixteen to one.....no....it's twelve to one now, that was the morning price, it's gone now, twelve to one, take it or leave it.....feckin' eejit....sorry Rory, this punter is giving me abuse-what's wrong? You still in the gaff?'

'I'm still in the gaff alright and I may stay where I am- I've no shoes!' said Rory.

'What?! You had them on last night when you came in didn't you?!' Michael quizzed not entirely seriously.

'Sure, I left them in your room when I came in steamed last night and then you locked your door,' said Rory becoming exasperated. Pause as Michael breaks into fits of laughter.

'Aye, you took them off last night when you came in,' remembered Michael.

'Have you a break from work anytime soon? Can you come down here with the keys and let me into your room?' asked an overwrought Rory, who was also now beginning to see the funny side of it.

Michael was still getting over it. 'Well I've bad news for you, I just took my break and I can't leave the store now 'cos one of the cashiers is out sick and I have to take bets here, hang on a sec...' A shaky punter approached the counter with a crumpled betting slip and presented it to Michael implying that it was a winning bet. Michael looked at the slip and recognising the name of a losing horse declares: 'No, that's a loser.'

'Where did he finish?' asked the shaky customer.

'He's still running!' said Michael. The punter was confused.

'He's still running? But the race was at 12 o'clock.'

'No, only joking, he came nowhere.... sorry Rory I have to go, it's mad busy here; the zombies keep coming at me! If you want the keys, you'll have to walk down here and get them!'

'What! In me bare feet?!' contested a surprised Rory, faced squarely with the hopelessness of the situation.

Rory grabbed his jacket and left Michael's flat shutting the door behind him with a frustrated bang. As he walked downstairs towards the main entrance of the building, he could hear the noise outside of a busy Pearse Street. Michael's landlord was a solicitor and owned not just Michael's flat but the whole building. He had an office downstairs, by the main entrance, where he spent most of his time.

Rory descended the stairs apprehensively and when he was at the bottom, noticed that the landlord was standing in his office looking through some letters. Eager to avoid a scene, he marched onwards towards the door but once there struggled with a bewildering doorknob.

The landlord heard his fumbles in the corridor and came out to be greeted by the grim sight of Rory looking like a man who had just emerged from the jungle. Rory looked at the landlord and the landlord looked at him. The landlord looked down at Rory's feet then up at him again. Nothing was said. Rory fumbled further with the doorknob but to no avail. The landlord, anxious to be rid of this unkempt individual, pushed the door release button.

Rory left the building barefoot and walked down the filthy street. It was bin day and the footpath was occupied by countless black refuse sacks which smelled of yesterday's dinner. He walked tentatively, aware of people regarding him suspiciously. There were comments from passers-by on the street:

'Where's he goin' with no shoes?' asked one Pearse Street resident as he opened his lunchtime can of strong cider.

'To the St. Vincent de Paul,' replied another.

'Bloody junkies!' remarked a passer-by to his wife. 'He probably sold his shoes for some heroin.'

'I'm having a bad day,' thought Rory, as he walked down the street. He had yet to pass the large Garda station, where he would have to explain himself to an officer of the law for sure if stopped. In all, it took him five long minutes to get to the bookies where Michael was waiting behind the counter, eager to see this degenerate of a human being enter.

Michael couldn't even look at him for the laughter as he dropped the house keys on the counter. The befuddled punters were more concerned with the 2:00 from Leopardstown than the sight of poor Rory. He left the bookies, feet now as grubby as a tramps vest and began another long barefoot walk back to the house to secure his shoes.

When Rory arrived back at the bookies, this time with his shoes on, Michael let him in to the employee area behind the counter which resembled a bank teller's work space. Rory sat for a while relaxing after his troublesome start to the day. His hangover reappeared, this time with renewed vigour. Michael continued working, taking bets from the endless stream of zombies. After a while Rory felt better and laughed with Michael about his bizarre morning. He was thinking that this might turn out to be a good day after all.

As they talked, a man suddenly approached the counter and began shouting. He produced a gun and pointed it at Michael, shouting 'Let me in!' Everyone froze. He shouted again: 'Let me in or I'll shoot!' Michael decided that he wouldn't take any chances and opened the door for the maniac.

Once inside the madman started waving the gun around wildly and shouting. 'You want to be shot? I'll shoot you all!' A flurry of chaos ensued as people screamed and left the store. 'Where's the safe?' demanded the crook. Michael pointed to his right. The robber raced over to it and found the door open but no money inside. All the money was sitting beside the till, where Michael had been counting it – a large wad of notes totalling about 3000 Euro.

While the crook was looking into the safe, Michael casually covered the cash with the *Racing Post* which was conveniently located close by. The robber couldn't believe that the safe was empty and continued to rant. Rory looked at the gun.

'Wait a minute,' he said, 'that's a water pistol!' He couldn't believe the neck on the man; to try and rob a bookie with a water pistol! The robber sensed his power rapidly fading. He wanted to get out of there.

There were some money bags filled with coppers near the counter each holding one or two Euro. Michael picked up the bags and handed them to the crook who took them looking rather frustrated. Knowing the game was up, he decided to run. He had secured the grand total of about 10 euro for his troubles. He left very unimpressed. Michael closed the shop immediately and called both head office and the Gardaí. He had saved the company over 3000 Euro, surely they would be appreciative?

Once finished explaining the event, Rory trying not to think about how grubby the soles of his feet were, turned to Michael and suggested "Mulligan's, for one?"

D'éirigh mé ar maidin a tharraing chun aonaigh mhóir
A dhíol 's a cheannacht mar dhéanfadh mo dhaoine romham
Bhuail tart ar a' bhealach mé 's shuí mise síos a dh'ól
'S le Siún Ní Dhuibhir gur ól mise luach na mbróg

From *Siobhán Ní Dhuibhir* (Traditional) as performed by Clannad

Translation:
I set out one morning for the big fair
Buying and selling as my people did before me
A thirst came upon me on the way and I sat myself down to drink
And with Susan O'Dwyer I drank the price of the boots

Blues, Birds and Bad English

I walked into Frank Ryan's at half 9 as the old-timer blues band was playing Bob Dylan's 'Meet me in the Morning.' Giovanni arrived in a few minutes later and in most un-Italian style, he made directly for the bar. We sat with two perfect pints of Guinness and listened to the blues.

Ryan's was a special bar; it was filled with vintage paraphernalia from old war boots to *bodhráns*. It served great pints but best of all they had the aforementioned blues band that did a Thursday night residency. Giovanni couldn't miss it such was his devotion to the blues.

I had made prior arrangements with The Man to pick up some party essentials. The dealer was an Italian cokehead who spoke Pidgin English on occasion and unintelligible gibberish the rest of the time. He wasn't the sort of fellow a young lady might present to her parents.

'I'd better call Silvio,' I said getting up.

'Why? You have to get some stuff?' asked Giovanni.

'Well I'd hardly call him to see how he was! Maybe invite him for a pint,' I replied sarcastically.

'Ha ha, no don't do that man!' Giovanni laughed.

Silvio was a rough sort of person. He would be there when he was good and ready, but at least he answered the phone unlike some other degenerate dealers.

'Dean is playing a gig tonight in

Whelan's at midnight. You want to come?' I asked Giovanni.

'He plays good stuff?'

'Yep, he's the business!'

'Ok, I go there man, I trust in you!' said Giovanni in his unique English.

The bar had stopped serving and people were finishing the last of their stout when Silvio finally arrived. He extended a hand and placed a huge chunk of Lebanese hash on my palm. Putting his finger to his cheek, he made the Italian *'buona'* hand gesture, to assure me of its quality. I gave him the money and said that I had to dash off to Whelan's to see another gig.

'Where is Whelan's?' he asked in Italian. After three years in Dublin, it was hard to believe that he could neither find his way around nor speak English. Giovanni was never happy to see Silvio but always forced a smile.

'I go with you,' said Silvio as we edged to leave. Giovanni and I exchanged disapproving expressions.

We began walking to the south side of the city, crossing the perpetually malignant River Liffey, going up Parliament Street and Dame Street before turning onto George's Street.

'Let's stop and roll a joint!' declared Silvio.

'No man! Is better to do and walk,' advised Giovanni with his usual errors. As we walked Giovanni had tobacco in one hand, hash in another, and a roach behind his ear. 'Give me a paper!' he demanded. We reached my house and instead of smoking it in the street, I advised that we step inside the hallway at least, to have some comfort. Giovanni puffed and passed it to Silvio, who was fiddling with a small package.

'You want *cocaina*?' he asked. I shook my head.

'You ever try?'

'Yeah I've tried it.'

'So you do with me, is good. *Ti giuro*,' persuaded Silvio.

'I don't do it man.'

'What you got bad time before? I got bad stuffs and bad time, but this is good. Pure stuff...you try!' No coke was pure, especially not in Dublin.

We finally went into the bar, hoping to catch the second half of the gig at least. Dean was on stage, shaking his bushy hair. His trusty acoustic guitar was plugged into a distortion pedal and from there into a loop station. He was layering melodies, riffs, chords and vocals. The drummer beat like a merciless Roman soldier going into battle. He seemed to be exorcising some ancient demons. Dean was so involved in the tune that he couldn't see anyone.

'Let's get a pint,' suggested Giovanni, 'they have good stuff here?'

'No, it's usually total shit, but let's drink it anyway.'

I looked over at Silvio and seeing the madness in his eyes I realised how coked up he was. He couldn't just carry that stuff around without taking it. He cornered Giovanni.

'*Tu devi aiutarmi stasera* (You have to help me tonight),' he said.

'*A fare cosa?* (To do what?)' said Giovanni allowing his dislike of the man to show just a little.

'*A vendere della cocaina.* (To sell some coke.)' Giovanni walked away.

'Man, that Silvio is crazy, totally crazy,' said Giovanni into my ear. He looked around and then continued: 'You know what he said to me just now? You know what he said?'

Silvio arrived with his wild eyes darting around, animal like. He rubbed his nose and started sniffing, trying to dislodge the coke stuck in his nostrils. He then began approaching random people who couldn't make out his bad English. I sensed danger with Silvio around. He had changed entirely since he took the latest few lines. The man was a liability. I went close to the stage to get away from him.

Dean blasted out his final song as I moshed like a possessed man to the sound of his distorted mayhem. Afterwards we shared a spliff outside.

'Dean, it's great to see you. You drove all the way from Galway to play a one-hour gig?'

'Yeah and I'm going back there now as soon as we get the stuff loaded into the van. The brother needs it tomorrow.'

Afterward I helped Dean and the drummer load up the guitars and amps. Sweat ran down his face as he ran to and fro, upstairs and down again.

'Ok, I'm off to Galway,' he said and gave me a man hug to say goodbye. It was 2am. Giovanni reappeared at my side.

'I finally lost him,' he said.

'Silvio?'

'Yeah, he's too much man, I never take a beer with him again. Man, you need to take the stuff and say: "Goodbye. I have to go meet someone, see you." You need to do like that.'

'I know, man. He's a danger.'

'He's trying to sell coke in there. I told him: "You can't do like you were in Italy." Here you can't do that stuff.' Giovanni was filled with rage and disappointment at having to spend his night babysitting this drugged up madman, keeping him out of trouble.

We took one more walk around the club looking at all the rock chicks doing their thing on the dance floor.

'Man, I have to go,' Giovanni announced suddenly, 'but I don't want that you have to leave. Stay man, maybe you find a woman.' Something clicked into place in my head and I decided to stay.

I walked around the bar and stood alone for a minute or so. Suddenly a bubbly brunette arrived and stood in front of me looking into my eyes.

'Hey! How are you?' she said as if she had known me for years. Her face was a picture of pure energy. I had never seen her before. 'What's your name?' she asked full of contagious enthusiasm.

'John,' I replied still intrigued by her fervour.

'I'm Sinéad'

'Where you from?'

'Kerry.'

'Cool.' I liked Kerry people once they

didn't mention football. 'Let's go outside.'

We began chatting and it appeared to be going somewhere.

'So you're a native Irish speaker?' I observed.

'Yeah, I speak it with my parents and friends at home.' We edged closer to each other.

'How long you been in Dublin?'

'Two years,' she replied, 'I love it up here.'

Out of nowhere, I heard a raspy voice.

'Oh man, *che fai*?!' Shit, it was Silvio. 'I thought you gone,' he croaked, stumbling a little. 'How are you?' he said to Sinéad giving her a slimy handshake.

'*Tá sé bun os cionn, ná labhair leis.* (He's in a mess, don't talk to him),' I advised her in Irish.

'You want roll joint?' he spluttered at me. We were standing at the entrance to Whelan's, two steps from the two middle-aged bouncers both of whom knew me well.

'No, man not here.'

'We roll joint now,' Silvio stated and began to look in his breast pocket for hash. He pulled out various rolling papers and pieces of cardboard instead. Next he produced the coke. He stood, swaying on the spot, for what seemed like an eternity, with a rock of coke the size of his thumb in full view.

'Man, put that shit away,' I urged him in Italian.

'I try find the hash,' he boomed so that everyone could hear him. People turned around to look.

I pressed him again and finally he put the coke away. The Kerry girl had been standing by getting a less than positive impression.

'*Tá an fear sin ar meisce.* (He's drunk),' I explained. It had been a long night and I was tired. I'd been spent speaking Italian to Giovanni for most of the night and now the change into Irish was too much for my brain.

'He is a little bit...' I started then realised that I had slipped back into Italian. She looked at me confused.

Silvio's ears cocked up. '*Lei parla italiano?!* (She speaks Italian?!)'

'*No, stavo provando a* ... (No, I was trying to...)' But Silvio cut me off.

'*Oh ciao bella! Mi capisci, sì? Sei troppo bella!* (Hi gorgeous! Do you understand me? You're too beautiful),' he said while gazing down her top. '*L'Italiano è bella come lingua, vero?* (Italian is a beautiful language, isn't it?)'

Sinéad looked at me confused. She spoke in Irish: '*Cad a duirt sé?* (What did he say?)'

'*Ceapann sé go bhfuil tú in ann caint as Iodáilis!* (He thinks you can speak Italian!)'

'*Ma, dove hai imparato, l'italiano?* (But where did you learn Italian?)' said Silvio directing his attentions to Sinéad, his pupils practically exploding.

'*No, lei non parla in italiano, ho sbagliato, io.* (No I made a mistake, she doesn't speak Italian.)' Silvio found this hard to grasp.

'*Cad a duirt sé?* (What did he say?)' asked Sinéad again quite confused. I had him speaking Italian into one ear and her speaking

Irish into the other and I was much too drunk to change between languages in subsequent sentences.

'*Tá sé go hiomlán ar meisce* (He's completely hammered),' I said, then losing control of my brain going back into Italian, '*è meglio...* (It's better...)'

'*Ah vero, parla italiano!* (I was right, she speaks Italian!)' Silvio in his state of drunken, coked-up ignorance, couldn't identify what was or wasn't Italian anymore.

'*Come mai parli italiano?* (How come you speak Italian?)' She gave him a confused look. As he talked he took out the large rock of cocaine again and held it in his hand. I wasn't sure what he was doing, neither was he.

'*Cad atá sé ag deanamh leis an rud sin?* (What's he doing with that?)' she asked.

There were no words.

'*An bhfuil sé do cara?* (Is he a friend of yours?)'

'*Níl, is fear mire é...eist liom, tá mé i mo chonaí ar an tsráid seo. Tá mo theach in aice linn. Ar mhaith leat dul ansin?* (No he's not. He's out of his mind...Listen, I live on this street. My house is near here. Do you want to go there?)'

'*Ceart go leor!* (Alright!)'

'*Seo linn.* (Let's go.)'

We left Silvio hovering drunkenly on the spot, talking to himself.

'*Cazzo, sono distruto...*(Shit, I'm destroyed.)'

'This is my gaff,' I told her and turned the key in the lock. We went in and shut the door. Upstairs she leaned in and I kissed her

I went into an ale house I used to frequent
I told the landlady my money was spent
I asked her for credit she answered me nay
Such custom as yours I can have any day

From *The Wild Rover* (Traditional) as performed
by Luke Kelly and The Dubliners

Wishbone

Tommy picked me up in a fine new Toyota something or other, which cost way too much money. It was not his of course, but borrowed from his trusting uncle. Being only seventeen, he probably shouldn't have been behind any wheel let alone that of such a luxury machine.

'You're welcome to come up here, there's a bed for you in the B+B,' Tommy had said on the phone. The proposition was tempting, a free stay in the B+B and a night 'on the tear.' In the countryside options weren't numerous and excursions lately had been few and limited in scope.

We were bound for Navan, hardly a metropolis, but bigger than where I lived. Just outside the town, we reached the newly built posh estate and zooming up the driveway, Tommy let her out a little. It was a wide road with a perfect surface, surrounded by a new lawn on both sides. The houses were all detached and well removed from each other and from the road. He knew the street well and there was never anyone on foot as all the residents were well off folk who never went anywhere unless it was in a car.

There was an 'S' bend in the road nearing the top of the hill, which the landscapers had put in as a design touch. Tommy showed off some slick manoeuvres to swerve through it at high speed before arriving promptly at the B+B's car park.

That night we made for the town,

stopping to eat some greasy take away en route. Tommy ordered his customary Snack Box, a feed of deep fried, breaded chicken with chips which had a distinct fishy savour.

Later we entered one of the town's finest and best known pubs, The Spider's Web, a grungy, rocked out sort of place where you sat in darkness.

Some of Tommy's acquaintances were propping up the bar and so we all sat around with pints of beer. Tommy was fond of Dave; he said he was 'the most well-adjusted ginger guy you'd ever meet.' We went through several rounds of beer when Tommy got it into his head that he had to find some smoke.

'D'you have any smoke, Dave?' he asked. Dave, quiet about such things, dodged the question. It was too late however, as once Tommy had this idea it couldn't be gotten rid of. He asked around in the bar bringing an unwilling Dave along. His efforts were met with no success.

The consensus at the bar was that tonight everyone should go to the nightclub.

'I'm not goin' to that shithole,' asserted Tommy, 'let's get some gange and head for the house.'

A little later, Tommy met Redser, another ginger guy, who promised to sell him some hash. Most of the lads were leaving for the nightclub by this stage and so was Redser when he finished his pint. Tommy checked his pockets, only a fiver. He 'legged it' back to the bar and gathered us all together with the news. Redser had hash for sale but alone he hadn't enough money to buy it - we had to pool cash. Conveniently, no one had any spare currency.

'Right I'll have to head back to the house and pick up some money,' said Tommy. 'I've the car here and I'll only be gone 5 minutes. Will you wait for me?'

'I will, yeah,' said Redser, 'I'll wait outside the bar for ya.' Tommy, Dave and I made for the car with haste. The atmosphere was electric with anticipation, with everyone chirping and laughing at the prospect of getting back into town to buy the hash. Seconds later we were starting up the hill towards the B+B. We came to the 'S' bend.

'Do what you did earlier, Tommy!' I encouraged. Tommy gripped the steering wheel determinedly and began to swerve the car in different directions. He was travelling much faster than when he had previously tried this. I smiled in excitement as we flew through the bend. At the final turn, Tommy had gone too wide and he struggled to reel the car back in. The sidewalk approached. I grimaced. There was an impact and the car flew over the kerb and into the fence where it finally stopped.

We were all shocked and struck dumb for several seconds. Dave was the first to move, opening the back door. Tommy sat for a moment before getting out and then made his way around to the passenger side, where the impact had occurred. I felt for the door handle, knowing that you shouldn't stay in a car after an accident. I tried to get out but the door opened just a few centimetres and no further. The lads were looking down at the front of the car. I crept across the gear stick and climbed out the driver's door. The lads weren't sure what was wrong and just looked at the wheel and then under the car.

The car had collided with the kerb first and then planted itself in the neighbour's fence. A light went on and out came a big man wearing pyjamas.

'Oh shit, that bollix of a cop is coming,' whispered Tommy without looking at him.

'He's a cop?' I asked.

'He's the head of the *Gardaí*, the top cop...the feckin' last thing I need.'

'What happened?' bellowed the big man when he arrived at the car. Smelling the drink on Tommy's breath he got suspicious. 'Does Tony know you have the car out?'

'Sure, a 'course he does,' said Tommy.

'My new fence is ruined,' the big man remarked quite resigned to the fact. 'Someone go get Tony!'

Tommy walked the one hundred metres or so down the road to the B+B where he found Tony stretched out in front of the TV with his wife. They seemed a world away, obviously not having heard anything.

Back at the car the cop asked me what happened. I gave as few details as possible.

'He took the bend too wide and didn't get her back in enough,' I explained.

'Were yis' going fast, yis' were?' prodded the cop.

'Oh, no, not too fast.'

Tony came stepping down the street with a look of horror on his face as he saw his brand new car wedged into the fence of his next door neighbour's house, the cop he hadn't wanted to annoy.

'Well Tom,' said Tony, holding it together, 'sorry about this.'

The car sat in a mess of broken wooden posts and recently planted shrubs. It slanted a little at the front and I pointed out that the passenger door wouldn't open. They looked down and saw that the panel above the wheel had been shoved into the door preventing it from opening. Looking closer, Tony sensed there was more amiss. He crouched down and examined the wheel, since it was turned to take the bend he could see behind it.

'Ah sure the bloody wishbone's gone!' Tony announced in frustration. He stared in woe at the axel seeing that it had been snapped straight across behind the wheel. This would be a big expense. 'How did you break the feckin' wishbone?' he asked Tommy.

'The wishbone's gone is it?' Tommy tried to be interested. He just knew that the car was screwed and that he wouldn't be driving it for a long while, if ever.

The cop crouched down in his pyjamas and had a look. 'Oh I see,' he exclaimed, 'she's snapped straight across.' He studied it a little longer and raised his head to look at Tommy.

'You had to be goin' a hell of a speed to snap the wishbone,' he said accusingly, slipping into police mode, and making an investigation.

'We won't be moving her,' said Tony, 'I'll have to ring the tow truck.' Then looking at the Garda's fence, he added: 'Sorry about the mess,

Tom.'

Tony was thinking of the potential bill, the wishbone would run into thousands and the panels were damaged too, not to mention the fence. Tony went to ring the tow truck. Tommy didn't want to be left with the cop and so nodding to Dave and me, we started to move towards the house. Tony was on his way back out now with news of the truck. His wife followed him in a dressing gown, shivering and moaning about the cold. Her eyes widened when she saw the scene: the cop in his PJ's looking sorrowfully at the carnage of his new fence and Tony, inconsolable at the sight of his fine new luxury car rammed into someone's garden.

In the house Tommy was swearing about not being able to get back in for the hash. 'He's probably waiting there still outside the pub,' he laughed.

He went into the sitting room and made for the liquor cabinet. 'Lad's are yis' havin' a drink?' he asked. We needed one after the incident. Dave sat down to indicate that he was game. Tommy raided Tony's alcohol, finding vodka and several large bottles of strong German beer. They were the expensive type that Tony had been saving. Tommy popped one pressing his two thumbs onto the metal top and passed it on to me. He grabbed the vodka bottle and immediately put it on his head downing several mouthfuls. It was only going one direction from here I thought.

Tony's wife came in an hour later and seeing Tommy's red face and drunken expression, she took the opportunity to press home some moral truths.

'Ah leave me alone, will ya?' he snarled and put the vodka bottle to his head again. It was bad timing. She walked out in a huff, giving up. Dave started to prod Tommy but he was beyond response. He staggered out of the sitting room and into a bedroom. He stumbled backwards towards the bed and swore some heinous oaths before collapsing completely.

At the Harvest Fair she'll be surely there
So I'll dress in my Sunday clothes,
With my shoes shone bright and my hat cocked right
For a smile from the nut brown rose.

From *The Star of the County Down* (Cathal McGarvey) as performed by John McCormack

The Numbers Game

'Do you want a cup of tea?' Pat asked when he walked into the room. Brendan sat pensively at the kitchen table.

'No!' he answered sharply. 'Yeah, alright.'

'What's wrong with you?' asked Pat as he calmly walked over to fill the kettle. He was in a relaxed mood. He'd spent all morning screwing his Swedish girl and now she had gone off clothes shopping and wouldn't be back for hours.

'Ahh, I did the dirt last night and I'm not too proud of me self,' said Brendan still looking into space.

'But sure you've done that plenty of times before!' laughed Pat. 'Who was she? Foreign?'

'Sure it doesn't matter. I shouldn't have done it.'

'Relax, will ya? That's not like you,' observed Pat as he searched for two clean mugs.

'Ah I know but this one's been around for a while, you know, and it's not right doing that on her.'

Brendan was clearly upset. He and his Polish nurse had been going out regularly for a few months and he had grown to feel something for her. The tea arrived, strong and beginning to darken the mug. Brendan took a sip and then decided:

'I'll have to break it off with her.'

'With who?' asked Pat. It was always

hard to be sure which girl Brendan was talking about.

'With the Polish girl, what do you mean "with who?"'

'Well you're a mysterious man!' commented Pat.

'No, that's it! I'll have to deliver the news to her tomorrow,' stated Brendan decisively.

'But sure, did you not say she's coming round this evening?' reminded Pat.

'Ah yeah, but I'll have to put her off, tell her some bullshit.'

'So who was the one last night then?' persisted Pat.

'Just some girl at the club. Irish. Ended up going back to her place. The usual carry on.' Brendan was sparing with the details.

'The usual carry on! Ha! Ha! You're some man for one man!'

*

He met Kasia, the Polish girl, for a quick coffee the next day and cut ties there and then. He made up an excuse instead of coming clean.

'We're getting too serious,' he had said. The poor girl was filled with sorrow. She sat sobbing in the café and wondered where she had gone wrong. Brendan, traumatised by the scenario, had to get out of there.

'I'm sorry. You're a lovely girl,' he added, heading for the door.

*

'I just couldn't look her in the face after doing the dirt, you know?' he told Pat later that evening.

'I think you're mad, she was a grand girl. I know well you'll be going mad around the town looking for another one by this time next week,' replied Pat, who'd evidently seen it all before.

Fast forward to next week and Brendan was on various internet dating sites drooling at the mouth searching eagerly for a replacement.

'Brendan, what are ya at?' Pat asked.

'I'm on the laptop, usin' d'internet.'

'Porn again?'

'You can shove your porn up your hole,' replied Brendan as he tried to concentrate.

'Looking for a ride,' he would shamelessly admit if you asked him; embarrassment was not something that pervaded his life.

He used dating sites, paid, free, every variety he could find. He searched tastelessly and indiscriminately for a girl that might be willing and game. Messages were sent and eventually some were received.

'It's a numbers game,' he reminded himself. 'The penny will drop, it will fall into place. It's only a matter of time.'

One girl replied with what seemed to be optimistic tones.

'Now you're talking!' he exclaimed. A few more messages and he asked her to meet, later that day.

She would be going later with a friend to the Laughter Lounge, she told him but he was welcome to come along if he was doing nothing else. He wasn't doing anything else. He was abundantly available for such invitations.

'I'll be wearing a red top,' he was advised in the message.

*

'Ho ho!' chanted Brendan as he walked down the hall.

'What's up with you?' asked Pat.

'I've got meself a date tonight,' he gloated.

'You cute hoor ya! How did you manage that?'

'Ah, it's a numbers game!' Brendan reiterated his motto.

'What did you do? Go on the internet?'

'Ahh! Numbers game!'

Later he put on his best jeans and made for town, walking down the quays to the Laughter Lounge.

'Ten Euro?!' he shouted at the bouncer. 'I've only got 20 on me and I want to get a couple of drinks in there too. Would you do it for a fiver?'

'No.'

'Where are you from? Poland? *Dobra! Kurwa!*' said Brendan.

'Ahh you know Polish swear words!' laughed the bouncer. 'Let this one in, he's a friend!' he instructed the cashier, a bored, stoned student. Only Brendan could, with basic words, engineer an opening.

'Ok,' said the Polish bouncer, 'have a good night.'

'*Dobra*,' shouted Brendan.

Once inside, he searched for a girl with a red top and he spotted about five. He sent her a message.

'I'm at the bar do you want a drink? Brendan.'

She replied: 'Ok, a vodka and coke. I'll meet you there.'

'Shit!' sighed Brendan, a vodka and coke would cost him about 9 Euro and with no guarantee of getting anywhere, it was a false economy.

She arrived full of beans and enthusiastic smiles. They talked rubbish trying to make each other feel comfortable. She was reasonably attractive but wore a slightly desperate look on her face. Brendan didn't mind.

He was invited to their table where her friend was sitting quite bored. They began a useless 3 way conversation in which Brendan endeavoured to gain their trust. At one point he noticed one girl look to the other to give a vague sort of affirmation of his good character. He looked out for such signs. He now knew it was on. Victory was within his grasp. The two girls left for a toilet chat. In there, he was mentioned more than once in-between motivational comments about her figure, how good she looked tonight, her choice of man and the justification of her actions. She was ready to proceed.

Brendan eyed the two girls as they returned from the toilet/discussion chamber. The friend would be leaving, she announced, as she had to work in the morning, you know how it is, etc.

Brendan was alone with his internet date that he had only encountered virtually that morning. It only took a simple 'Would you like to come back for a cup of tea?' and they were leaving together.

The friend stayed just long enough to see if I was alright and then she was game ball, Brendan concluded privately.

Back at the ranch and Brendan was making the tea. She didn't seem to want it though once he put it on the table. She asked which room was his and soon began dragging him there while taking his shirt off.

'Holy smoke,' thought Brendan, 'I met a wily one tonight!'

He went into the room with her and laid her on the bed. After a bit of fondling she was ready for the main course.

'Wait!' shouted Brendan. He dashed naked across his room and picked up his bicycle helmet.

'Put this on!' he advised.

'Why?' she asked. 'Am I going for a ride?!'

'You sure are!'

He wouldn't begin until she put on the helmet.

'What are you gonna do to me?!' she asked tying the strap.

'I'm gonna give you the ride of your life!'

*

Next morning Brendan came strolling into the kitchen, shoulders back, looking relaxed. Pat was there already.

'Cup of tea?' Brendan asked with a smile.

'Aye! You cute hoor! I don't know how you do it!'

'Did I not tell ya it's only a numbers game?!'

Oh of all the money that e're I spent
I spent it in good company
and of all the harm that e're I've done
alas it was to none but me.

From *The Parting Glass* (Traditional) as
performed by Liam Clancy and Tommy Makem

Carl the Chef Evades the Cops

eejit: n. Irish slang for stupid person

Carl the chef sat on the sofa, game controller in hand and eyes on the screen. He looked over at Joey, who was concentrating on the ashtray.

'Giz a drag a dat, hi! You've been bogarting it long enough,' ordered Carl.

'Hold your horses, will ya?! Sure, I only lit it a minute ago.' Joey handed the joint to Carl.

Carl the chef and Joey sat around most nights in their run-down 2-bed flat in Phibsboro, on Dublin's north side. Carl was really a chef, but had been enjoying a lengthy break from the hot kitchen. Joey had no idea what he was.

The phone rang. Joey looked at the name before answering.

'It's Micko, he probably wants some hash...How are ya Micko? No, just chilling here at the gaff. No, I won't be down for a pint tonight. Hmm...no we don't have anything to spare, Micko. We've only a wee lump for ourselves. Try the lads up at the towers, they always have a bit lying around. Alright Micko, take it easy, bye.'

'That lad's always askin' us for hash,' said Carl refocusing on the screen.

'I had two birds on to me earlier as well, man. The whole a Dublin's mad lookin' for hash!'

Carl took a break from his game to enjoy

a moment of revelation.

'Here, Joey! Why don't we start knocking out a bit ourselves? Everyone's always asking us for it, we'd have it all gone in no time.'

'Ah me bleedin' head'd be wrecked with the phone goin' all the time.'

'Yer man Anto, could get us a nine-bar, handy enough. We'd be smokin' for free and we'd make a few quid,' insisted Carl.

'It'd be nice to always have a bit around,' agreed Joey coming round to the idea.

'Here, you have Anto's number there don't ya? Give him a call.'

Joey picked up the rolling papers. 'I'll call him after I make a joint.'

'Ah go on, call him now. You'll be too stoned to talk to him after.'

*

A few nights later Carl and Joey sat on the sofa as usual, this time with a huge chunk of Moroccan hash in front of them. Carl had been eager to begin testing it. While particularly stoned and looking at the nine-bar, paranoia got the better of Joey.

'Here, Carl...What if the cops come in?'

'Ah man, don't be freakin' me out, will ya? There'll be no bother from the Guards.'

'Philly got busted last month,' Joey reminded him.

'Jaysus give it a rest man. We can just hide it,' Carl decided.

'Hide it?' considered Joey, 'Ok, ok, we'll hide it...it'll be grand.' Joey began to calm. This lasted for a moment and he puffed and examined the ashtray as usual. The paranoia kicked in again.

'What if they bring in the dogs?' Joey persisted.

Carl looked over at him and then back at the huge piece of hash in front of him. He felt the stress building. He thought about it and then he realised he had a point.

'Shite, you're right! They'll find it,' Carl concluded.

'I know, no shit they'll find it!' said Joey.

They worried for a few moments, too paranoid to think, even to turn on their games console. Joey studied the ashtray again searching for inspiration. Just then he had a eureka type moment and exhaling quickly he began to chatter excitedly.

'Let's break up little bits of hash and put it all around the place. We can put it on the carpet and in the hall so that when the dogs come in they'll be confused. They won't know where to look!'

'That's genius!' exclaimed a red eyed Carl.

They immediately began breaking off little chunks from the nine-bar. Both got down on their hands and knees and began spreading small crumbs around on the floor. They scattered it well and sat down satisfied at their good work

Carl lay back and lit up a big joint to celebrate a job well done.

'The dogs'll never get it now,' concluded a satisfied Carl.

'The feckin' dogs'll be goin' round in circles!' laughed a stoned Joey, and he began

crawling around erratically on the floor making howling noises befitting a confused canine.
*

One and a half stoned weeks later the phone rang.

'Naw, Micko we don't have an'thin' left to sell. We've only a wee lump for ourselves.'

Joey put down the phone and looked at Carl.

'We've only enough left for 2 joints,' grumbled Carl.

'U serious?!' asked Joey. 'Last time I looked there was a big lump on the table, did you smoke it all ya eejit?!'

'What the hell are you giving out to me for? You're the one that gave them birds a quarter for free!' rattled Carl.

'They were hot man!' pleaded Joey.

'Yeah but you didn't even get near that one in the end. You're the feckin' eejit!' asserted Carl the chef as he reached for the rolling papers.

Two or three minutes passed and nothing changed.

'Let's call Philly or Alan the Doss,' suggested Joey finally.

'Philly's locked up, ya eejit.'

'Well, we'll call Alan then?'

'Ok you call him though; he hates me.'

Joey rang the number. No answer.

'He's not pickin' up. He must have nothin'...balls to it!'

'Let's smoke the last bit.'

'Ahh save it man, it's only 7, it'll be a long night'.

Two minutes later they smoked it anyway.

A frustrated couple of hours later and the tiny remaining speck of dope had long been smoked. Joey rang the number again. Still nothing, his phone was off. It didn't look good.

'Feck it he's not gonna answer now, it's too late,' grumbled Joey.

With no more gange left and no answer from the dealer Joey went from restless to hopeless. Then he remembered something.

'What about all that stuff we scattered around on the floor last week when we got the nine-bar?'

'Oh yeah!' said Carl, 'that was your idea, ya muppet!'

'Let's try and pick up the bits!' screamed Joey.

With that he got up and began crawling around the floor like a confused canine once again, searching through pieces of pizza crust, dirt and hair on the floor.

'Give me a hand man!' yelled Joey.
Carl got down on his knees also.

'I think I got a bit!' said Joey as he separated pieces of fluff and pubic hair from something so miniscule that it was barely visible.

'I got something,' said Carl. 'Ah shit, it's only a pebble!'

*I will arise and go now, for always night and day
I hear lake water lapping with low sounds by the
shore;*

From *The Lake Isle of Innisfree*, a poem by
William Butler Yeats

The Guarana Night

The front door opened at 3am and I heard the commotion of many drunken people straggling in. As luck would have it, I had been devouring a bottle of Chianti and wasn't ready to sleep anyway. My flatmate, Dave, entered with a boisterous bunch of 'head the balls' he had rounded up from the pub. The room filled immediately with conversation.

There was Aiden, wild and prone to sudden bouts of lunacy, his English girlfriend, well-oiled and ready for more and several others I'd never seen before. Lydia was a slim, distant-looking girl with long brown hair. I knew her only by reputation. She had an appetite for booze and drugs which was as immense as his. She didn't speak, instead extended a hand.

Aiden rang Mossy the Dealer, a friend who lived close-by and had been specialising in MDMA for the past few months. He asked if he wanted to go to 'a cool party in Dave's house.'

His ploy was to entice him over hoping he would bring along some party powder. So desperate was Aiden for the stuff, he thought he'd better ask Mossy to bring along a good amount to be on the safe side. 'You might want to bring along, you know...' Mossy knew exactly what to bring.

While Aiden was anxiously awaiting the arrival of The Man he became somewhat strung out. He called him again 15 minutes later.

'Are you coming? Cool... where are you now?...Man, just hop in a taxi and you'll be here quicker. Fuck it, it's only a fiver!' Mossy was walking because drug dealer or not, the distance was too short in his opinion to justify a cab.

In the sitting room where 6 of us now sat, Dave produced a bottle of Jameson but no glasses. I offered to get some but he suggested that the bottle might be gone by the time I'd come back. Sitting on the sofa with Aiden's gathered drug fiends, he opened the bottle and putting it on his head, took a long drink. The bottle was passed on and so continued the desecration of good whiskey. I sat opposite and when the bottle arrived, put a measure into a glass so I could at least admire the amber colour while I drank. I handed the bottle to my left where Aiden and his bird were seated. Both took good gulps and soon it returned to Dave, now almost half empty.

The doorbell rang and Aiden bounced out of his seat like a yoyo. He dashed over to let Mossy in, welcoming him with a manly hug. Mossy had been expecting a party but when he entered he was disappointed to see just a few drunks on a sofa with Aiden's girl being the solitary female. He was glad he hadn't taken a taxi.

'Did you bring the stuff?' Aiden's eyes asked. Mossy wanted to be appreciated for his personality not just his MDMA and so first sat down on the sofa to get acquainted. Finally getting impatient, Aiden had to ask him for it.

Mossy took out a few bags of white powder and laid them on the table. 'This is all good stuff,' he confirmed as he arranged them in order of quantity. 'This one is 50...and these are

50 too or there's this one for 70.' Aiden's eyes screamed for a hit. His pupils darted from one bag to another, he couldn't decide, he wanted all of them.

'Lad's, will we get two bags? There's loads of us here.'

'Ah now buddy, sure won't one do ya?' said Dave.

'Well we'll get the big one then. Have you any cash?' he asked, then turning to me: 'John, are you gonna chip in?'

'I'm fine with my whiskey,' I said. The others took out twenty Euro notes as Mossy waited patiently, eying the money. Aiden straightened himself up in the sofa and tucked in his long legs. Lydia moved a little closer to the table to see the action. Mossy took his money and passed the bag to Aiden.

Lydia now observed closely as Aiden opened it with care, mindful of its precious contents. The others were more relaxed about the whole scene and content to converse quietly, although still aware of the significance of the moment.

'I heard someone say that the best moment of any drug is the one just before you take it,' I said to the group. They ignored me and instead regarded Aiden as he prepared to delve into the contents.

'We'll all just stick our fingers in and take a bit, alright?' he said as he wet his finger slightly and dabbed it into the powder. A finger covered in white re-emerged from the bag and he thrust it into his mouth. He rubbed his gums gently and made a stupid grin before handing the bag on to Lydia, who had positioned herself at his elbow. The bag went round the group just as the whiskey had done, with everyone tasting its unknown contents. Mossy took some and licked his lips quickly afterwards, in a manner befitting one accustomed to such things. While some sat back to reflect and observe changes in their brains, Mossy the MDMA pro, began to talk to me about music.

'I saw your guitar there, do you play much?' For him the drug was having less effect as he had been ingesting it daily off and on for weeks. Aiden wasn't far behind him on this and often went into work in the transport office, well and truly caned. No wonder the transport system is in such a state.

Aiden lay back into the couch and stretched his legs out. Lydia moved in close to him and he put his arm around her. They turned their backs on the rest of the group. Dave seemed completely unfazed by the narcotic and merely sat still with a vague smile on his face. Mossy continued to chat, saying that he had tried many times to play the guitar but he had always given up.

'Doesn't it hurt your fingers?'

'No, that stops after a few weeks if you keep at it.'

'What about The Beatles, they're easy to play aren't they?'

'Not really. Some of them are easy alright but The Beatles were seriously good musicians. They used some strange chords and lots of changes.' This seemed to satisfy him for the moment. I took a sip of the whiskey. The atmosphere in the room had changed. Most people were on edge and their eyes darted around restlessly. Others were slightly sedated but happy and chatty. Aiden and his bird had begun to make out on the couch, gently but passionately.

Upstairs, Jane, the only girl living in the house, slept soundly. Since moving in just a few days ago she had only spoken to us twice in the form of quick chats at the bottom of the stairs. Sound travelled through the house like there were no walls and everything the maniacs said could be heard upstairs.

The bag of MDMA was attacked for a second time. It was now running low and once it had done the circle of the table it ended up where it had started, in Aiden's hands. He put it into his mouth and licked and sucked it, like a baby with a soother. Once it was completely licked clean he cast it away onto the table, covered in saliva. The room once again went silent for a few minutes as each had their own private moment of ascension. Once all were high again they chattered relentlessly. Aiden and Lydia went back to making out. They got more passionate and Lydia rolled over on top of him. We glanced over briefly and went back to chatting.

'Dave, do you mind if we go to your room?' Aiden asked, 'Lydia's tired. She wants to lie down.'

'Sure, go for it,' agreed Dave. They left, really high. Being the only one not off his head on white powder, I was getting bored. I looked at the time - 4am.

A few minutes passed and then we heard sudden noise and commotion upstairs. Dave got to his feet and dashed up to investigate. At the top of the stairs he found the door to his room propped open and Lydia lying on the hallway floor, topless and wriggling like a fish. Aiden, meanwhile, was jumping on the bed like a child. Dave said nothing and walked on past to the bathroom. When he came out Aiden was dragging Lydia to her feet. She hopped around like a kangaroo before scurrying into the room. She was bananas.

Downstairs the conversation was becoming faster, as everyone was flying on their own separate yet inclusive buzz. We heard groaning from upstairs. Lydia was making sounds of intense pleasure. It got louder and louder until she was practically screaming. Poor Jane in the other room was surely woken up with the abundant wailing but didn't complain. Lydia's grunting continued. It seemed as if she would never come although she was definitely teetering on the edges of it. Finally there was quiet and the conversation was restored. It was 5am.

The whiskey bottle was drained and placed on the table beside the empty, sticky drug bag, which Aiden had been sucking. 70 Euro had gone in an hour. Mossy took out another bag and asked if anyone was interested. No one spoke. 'My shout,' he confirmed. Suddenly there were murmurs of approval on learning that they did not have to pay. 'Well I'll have just a little bit more,' said one. 'Ah yeah, just wee bit,' said another.

As Mossy opened the bag, the sounds of passion were heard again from upstairs. Aiden was really giving it to her. She moaned in delight. Her moans were first moans of pleasure but then became more urgent wails of imminent climax. But she did not come; she wallowed in this near climax stage for what seemed like ages. Jane was still getting no sleep that was for sure. Finally there was silence and the lads laughed, musing about what an animal Aiden was.

'Mossy, you used to live with him;' said one, 'is he always like this?' Mossy nodded.

'The man is an anomaly, a force of nature.'

Mossy went upstairs to use the toilet and was surprised to see Lydia running around the corridor knickers half on, bra on the floor. He went back downstairs and had a slash in the garden instead.

No one wanted to go home while free drugs were being handed out. The endless chatter continued and when Aiden and Lydia commenced their third bout of banging and wailing, no one even mentioned it.

At some stage I gave up my vigil and went to bed. The mad couple were silent now and I was able to get some sleep. When I awoke it was the afternoon and everyone was gone. I was standing around downstairs looking at the mess and unmistakable evidence of a wild night when Jane arrived home. Oh no, I thought. I'll have to explain all this to her. She gave me a knowing smile and didn't even complain. This was a good response, as any drama now would have taxed my already taxed brain.

'Get much sleep?' I asked cheekily.

'No, there was some noise in the room beside me.'

'Ahh that, yes. Dave let his friend use his room.'

'Ahh! So it wasn't Dave then? I was going to say I wouldn't be able to look him in the face again.'

'No, Dave was downstairs the whole time.'

'What a guy Dave's mate is!' she mused. 'He's a machine! There were a series of peaks there!'

My phone rang. 'Hey John? It's Aiden.'

'Good man, how you getting on today?'

'Weary man, weary. Listen, did you see my phone around? Will you look up in Dave's room?'

I went upstairs, opened the door and regarded the zone of debauchery. Bed clothes were tossed everywhere and the pillows were on the ground. I searched for the phone.

'Yeah, it's here man.'

'Great, I'll pop over later. Thanks man!'

My eyes were drawn to the bedside table. Evidence of last night was left conspicuously in full view: an empty pack of condoms and the remains of a box of guarana, herbal energisers. It seemed a suitable partnership for his evening of hell-for-leather activity.

From Bantry Bay up to Derry Quay
And from Galway to Dublin town
No maid I've seen like the brown cailín
That I met in the County Down.

From *The Star of the County Down* (Cathal
McGarvey) as performed by John McCormack

One Night Walkabout

Brian never had a one night stand and was curious as to what the etiquette might be. He had seen many American movies though, and erroneously assumed that art would reflect life. He expected a scenario whereby, he would wake up as the sun peaked through his curtain, to see that the object of his desires had now vanished into thin air, parting without even a note. Surely this would be the reality he daydreamed, as he returned to his dorm room.

A young student in his second eye-opening year at Trinity College Dublin, Brian was eager to experience something of college life that might meet his preordained expectations. Through intelligence and introversion he had been offered accommodation on campus, which is reserved for the select few. Trinity College's central location was convenient for him as he was the type that had always a coffee in hand and someone to go and meet. He was in need of constant polite and carefully crafted conversation, such was his nature. From this central location, he would pop into one of the two bars on campus to see what was happening or wander up to O'Donoghue's for some decent trad music, sampling the myriad of wonders the city centre had to offer.

One night he attended a fellow Trinity student's graduation party in the Hairy Lemon, a drunken stagger from Grafton Street. Once there he began to notice the large number of attractive girls around and his libido informed him that he should go talk to one of them. The graduation party included a mixture of friends and random people connected to the alumni. He succeeded in developing only protracted conversions with some friends as he gazed around the room. Just then it happened, a meteor hit the Earth, a ray of light illuminated the grey, he saw a goddess.

She stood resting her shapely arms on a table while conversing with a friend. She had long dark hair, a slim and delicate figure which was covered by an exquisite black dress. She sipped a gin and tonic from a long glass and smiled as her friend related something of amusement. He nudged a girl from his class, asking: 'Do you know that girl in the black dress?'

'Sure! Do you want an introduction?'

He was soon speaking to said goddess and her friend. Both girls were English and had just begun studying at Trinity College. It turned out that they had friends in common so he wasn't really a total stranger to them. Cathy and Rachel were pleased to make his acquaintance. The latter was the object of his desires, and it turned out that he knew her by reputation. He was besotted and proceeded to spend the next hour desperately trying to seduce her by any means possible.

He ignored Cathy, the other English girl, who stood close by the entire night, looking mostly at the ground. Brian's laboured attempts to win Rachel's affection were failing miserably but still he kept trying, in the end he had tried everything but came away with nothing.

Soon the bar had closed and the night was at an end when Cathy, the girl whom he had barely spoken to, asked him something out of the blue.

'Brian, you live on campus, could I sleep on your couch tonight? It would save me the trouble of going all the way back to Rathfarnham,' she explained. 'I have a lecture at 9am. It would be such a long journey to go to sleep for just a few hours.' He agreed immediately.

The only problem was that the girl in question was not the one he had been tripping over himself to impress all night. He eventually had to accept defeat in his bid to 'score' and was soon accompanying the quieter, smaller girl to his room on campus.

'We don't have a sofa,' he informed her at last, 'but there is lots of space, if you don't mind sharing the room?' She didn't mind.

As his location was right in the centre of town, he often got asked to provide this service, and was currently more popular than ever. They reached the halls of residence and he led her up the steps to his corridor, where 8 people lived, each with their own room. He went into his room and pulling together some blankets and pillows he formed a make-shift bed on the floor. He invited her in and being a gentleman, suggested that she take the bed.

As he fiddled dutifully with blankets she suddenly threw herself at him. She began to press herself against his chest as he reeled backwards in shock.

He was being seduced by a shy girl who was evidently going after what she wanted.

His mind measured the situation: he'd never had a one night stand before but maybe was about to participate in his first. He thought he could handle what might be involved as American movies had prepared him well. They probably wouldn't talk much in the future, it could be perfect. The evidence was conclusive. He allowed nature to take its course in the end and was soon sleeping soundly.

He woke up in the middle of the night and looked around the room. He noticed that all of his clothes were in a pile near the foot of the bed, while all her clothes were scattered around the room. He had ripped them off her passionately, in his best attempt to recreate a Hollywood scene. Her clothes were there but she wasn't. She was gone from the bed and from the room.

He thought again about the movies and how one night stands are depicted: a night of unbridled passion with one person disappearing discreetly early in the morning, before the other wakes up. But they didn't usually leave naked.

He got up and unsure of what to do, looked down the corridor for clues. Nothing. He picked up all her clothes from around the room, and hesitating, put them into a plastic bag. He got dressed and went outside. It was around 5am on a Monday morning in a cold Irish November. He wandered around the campus of Trinity College, searching for a confused, probably naked girl.

He walked out onto Front Square and

was alone there in the eerie morning. He checked the secretary's office but no one was there. He did a full trip of the campus - out to the rugby pitch by the Pavilion bar and back through New Square to where he had started his search. He couldn't see her anywhere and there was nobody around to even ask. He was worried.

Just then he remembered that he had the phone number of a friend of hers. He hesitated though; it was 5.30am and she would be asleep. What was he going to say anyway? 'I lost your friend. Oh, by the way she's naked!' He thought about calling the Garda as there was a station nearby on Pearse Street. He hesitated again and thought that he would probably get locked up. Let's face it; he was walking around Trinity College at half 5 in the morning with a bag of women's clothes asking if anyone had seen a naked girl. Cold and tired, he decided to return to his room, in case she turned up there.

When Brian returned to the corridor he stood around dejected for a few minutes before deciding to make a cup of tea. Everything is better after a cup of tea. While waiting for the kettle to boil, his mind ran over the night before. He thought about some of the things she had said during their wild encounter. 'Teach me some manners!' 'I need to be punished!' were some of the more memorable ones.

Just then he heard a noise which startled him out of his early morning daydreams. He recognised it as the sound of the fire exit closing. He looked down the corridor and there, as naked as the day she was born, stood his one night stand. She was wandering around at the end of the corridor, looking confused. Brian stood for a moment aghast, unable to believe his eyes. She approached one of the bedrooms and pausing for a moment, began knocking on the door.

'Brian?!' she inquired, 'I'm looking for Brian!' She turned to the next door and began knocking. "Where is Brian's room?" Brian, seeing what was happening, began running towards her. He didn't want to shout in case someone woke up. Just then the first door opened and a sleepy girl came out and was surprised by what she saw. Another door opened, this time it was a guy who came out. His jaw dropped. Brian stood there and with the bag of clothes in one hand, trying to reassure everyone that things were fine, just fine.

Cathy, however, was still naked, confused and in the corridor. Brian ran to his room and grabbed a jacket. He ran back out and threw it over Cathy and marched her back to his room as quickly as possible. He stopped briefly to reassure the now sizable collection of flatmates.

'She's grand, she just got a little lost that's all! Don't worry its fine...' But it would not be fine; flatmates never think the same of you again after seeing you publicly 'rescue' a naked girl in the corridor. Back in the room he looked for answers.

'What the hell were you doing wandering around naked?' he asked her. She recounted that she had found herself standing on the stairs of the emergency exit without any clothes on. Worse still, she couldn't remember how she got there or the way back. She had then proceeded to wander around trying to find something familiar so as to establish where she was. Then a name had appeared in her head: 'Brian! Yes that's it! That's who I came here with.'

She had been looking for his room after that, knocking on doors and calling out his name. Also being English and a recent arrival, she didn't know Dublin or the university very well. In the dark, the campus seemed a maze. She eventually found her way back to his corridor, cold and confused. She had apparently been sleep walking, something she confessed to doing now and then, though usually not naked.

Brian thought about the conversation he might have with his flatmates later that day and shivered. He dreaded who else might hear about this as the day progressed. He would probably get a reputation, or at least a nickname.

He gave her a cup of tea and sent her to her early lecture. He would not forget his first one night stand. Hollywood had not prepared him, he reflected. His views on the subject seemed to be galvanised, as he has opted for long term relationships ever since.

Tharla isteach i dteach mé
Is casadh orm daoine
D'fhiafraigh siad mo ainmse
Cén tír inar tógadh mé
Dúirt mé leo i mBéarla
Gur tógadh mé in Éirinn
Láimh le Loch Eirne
I gCoillidh Lios na Raoch

From *An tOileán Úr* (Traditional) as performed by
Clannad

Translation:
I happened into a house
Where I met some people
The asked my name
What country I was born
I told them in English
That I was born in Ireland
By the side of Loch Eirne
In the woods of Lios na Raoch

Campus in Three Acts

Act One: The Balloon Man

We met at the Forum Bar. It was so called because the bland concrete exterior apparently bore a vague resemblance to a Roman Forum. It was the secondary bar on campus, frequented only by post-grads and older students. Dean was typically full of beans.

'How're ya horse?' he asked inquisitively. Dean was a country lad of about 25, tall, but not lanky, wearing a healthy week's worth of unkempt beard and a Moroccan-style jacket. He was of restless nature, which rendered him uplifting rather than grating. We exchanged caveman pleasantries for a moment while watching the other students come and go.

Some sci-fi guys were preparing an outdoor projector for their society movie night. We stood around talking about nothing with them for a few minutes then we heard a voice behind us.

'Do you want a balloon?'

Out of nowhere emerged a peculiar individual speaking with an English accent. He looked strangely at ease, as if he was speaking to us from the restful position of a particularly comfortable armchair. He spoke with an exceptionally strong cockney accent; a sound most unusual in South Dublin.

'Do you want a balloon?' he repeated.

We looked at him confused. He then drew our attention to the large gas canister which was at his feet. Now more confused still, we stared at this canister and back at him. Was he going to make balloon animals?

'No thanks, you're grand man!' said one student.

'I'm not interested man,' said another before one of the society folk stepped forward.

'How d'ya do it?' asked Sci-fi Dude No.1.

'I'll show you,' replied the smiling stranger.

We watched as he produced the aforementioned balloon and began to fill it with gas from the large canister. When it was full he grasped it excitedly.

'I've done 15 of these today,' he informed us. 'It just feels great man, it totally relaxes you.'

He put the balloon to his lips and inhaled furiously until it was empty. He then exhaled back into the balloon, blowing it up again. He repeated this several times. Soon he will stop, I thought, after he had taken several breaths. He continued determinedly as his face began to change color and he started to lose consciousness. But still he did not stop.

He inhaled the gas from the balloon and exhaled back into it. His legs drooped and he became unsteady. People looked on wide-eyed. He inhaled and exhaled one or two more straddled breaths and then he finally stopped.

He took the balloon from his mouth and gleaming all over said: 'You gotta try it lads!'

Hardly a good advertisement I thought, but still Sci-fi Dude No.1 stepped forward.

'I'll take one.'

'Ok twenty Euros!' demanded the

Balloon Man impatiently.

'Ha?'

'Yeah, twenty man.' It was 2008 and he was taking advantage of the final days of the economic boom in Ireland.

'I'll have some too' interrupted Sci-fi Dude No.2.

They pooled money and handed over notes to the weird stranger.

He filled a pink balloon and Sci-fi Dude No.1 accepted it gratefully, wet at the lips (and probably behind the ears) he ripped into it. It hit him quickly. He began by inhaling rapidly as the Balloon Man had done, but quickly reduced the frequency of his breaths and was clearly struggling. The Balloon Man urged him on: 'U gotta do it for longer man!'

Sci-fi Dude No.1 tried to continue and managed a few more breaths before throwing in the towel. Retreating from the scene, he was as deflated as the pink balloon he had just discarded. He could be seen looking into the distance, bewildered, like a maniac.

'How was it man?' asked another sci-fi guy. 'Oh yeah, it's great man!' answered the lost sailor in a completely unconvincing way.

Victim No.2 stepped forth. We left. It was not balloon time for us.

'Flying saucers,' murmured Dean, 'that sci-fi lad was all over the place.' I glanced back in time to see the cockney hand over another shiny pink balloon.

Act Two: A cup of tea

'Do you want a cup of tea?' enquired

Dean. He wasn't referring to the famous Indian beverage popularized during colonial times.

'Ok, let's roll it in the Arts block.'

'Let's do it in the Film office!' Dean suggested eyes wide.

'Ohh I don't know. Ok let's do it!'

He had keys to the room that the Film Society used to drink tea and create in-jokes. We unlocked the door and went in, immediately switching on the huge Mac to hear some tunes. While it was booting up, Dean impatient as ever, grabbed his guitar which was on the seat beside him and played a bizarre sequence of chords and melody which could be described as: Bob Marley meets an Indian while they were both high on petrol.

Next door was the newspaper office. The folk in there never went home early, they needed all the hours of the day to groan and speak in typically high tones. They could hear everything through the paper walls and wouldn't approve of comments such as: 'Man, this tea is fierce sticky!' We had to keep it on the down low.

'Let's go to the lake!' proclaimed Dean.

We left the Arts block and stepped forth towards the central part of campus. We passed the library where some stereotypical 'D4' girls were gathered. Dean stopped to tie his shoelace. We could hear the girls' conversation:

'He was a dirty knacker, Aoife, you shouldn't text him back!' said one.

'Yeah, I don't like talking to these 'boggers,' they are so stupid like. Get a life, Dublin's better than the bog, like!' said another.

Dean was disgusted; still he was not

concerned or interested by their musings. To them he was also a dirty knacker and he knew it. That's why he kept to his own kind. He was accepted by country people, Dublin's north siders, and the Spanish and Italian communities. The D4 people were on a different wavelength.

To explain: D4 is the postal district on the south side of Dublin where the most expensive land in Ireland is located. The area has a perceived sense of upward mobility. The 'D4' guys and girls are actually mostly from the south County Dublin region, near to, but outside of Dublin 4. The area consists of smart housing estates with high price tags near coastal villages such as Blackrock and Killiney.

The area's emerging younger generation are distinguished by their unusual accent often described as 'Mid-Atlantic.'

Unfortunately, they are resented uniformly by everyone living elsewhere in Dublin and the country. This comes out of a mixture of jealousy at their fortunate circumstances (don't worry Daddy will pay for it!) and a genuine dislike for their elitism and fickle nature. The stereotype suggests that all guys from this area are clad only in rugby related clothing and branded casual wear. They walk tall and speak about irrelevant matters.

The girls on the other hand are partial to wearing several inches of makeup and a variety of skirts and tops intended to showcase their orange-tinted, fake tanned skin. Several bottles of fake tan are needed to affect this look, still they neglect to apply it effectively and leave white areas and finger streaks. Some manage to look vaguely human, others even look good.

The most essential part of the "D4 look" has to be the dyed blonde hair (the guys are guilty of this also). It seems that there are no genetic explanations for the huge occurrence of blonde-hair among people in south Dublin.

Act Three: 'D'ye wanna get in de van?'
The campus centrepiece is a nasty lake which is set into concrete. Some swans and ducks peruse the stagnant waters.

'The swans will never leave,' Dean commented, 'but that's because the powers that be have clipped their wings.'

Out of sight of the library and the Arts block, Dean sparked up the joint and began to talk of a girl he had begun to engage with. Imagine an unrestrained, enthusiastic Irish country accent:

'I played a gig in that bar down the country last Saturday night as usual. But there's this foxy barmaid working there and I knew she was up for something. But you know, I play there and she's the one who pays me, so I didn't do nothing.'

He took a toke of the joint and glanced over at some more D4 girls that were passing.

'But she comes to me at the end of the night and says: "Do u wanna go smoke a joint?" So I said "Yeah, I'll get the van."'

He had an old van which he used sometimes to move music equipment around. It was not luxurious, not even close.

Dean on the van: 'Ah she's just about

road worthy, no more, she's plain and gritty. Still she helped us out of many hobbles and got us home on many dark nights.'

He continued: 'I took her to the lake outside of town and we smoked a joint. But sure, you know, one thing led to another and the next thing she was taking off her clothes. Then the van was shaking.'

'We were out there for hours, man. Eventually I left her home and she had to creep into her house so not to wake up her folks. Then I had to drive the 40 miles home, that's after doing a gig and being with her all night. I was exhausted man.'

He took a puff and exhaled through his nose.

'But I don't know what to do man, you know, she's a nice girl but I gotta play in the bar. I think I should just end it, man. But I don't know...man we were banging in the van for ages and she was really DIRTY... you know, dirty girl...' Dean gazed into the middle distance reminiscing for a moment.

'It could be fun man. You know, livin' on the edge, shagging after the gig. Could be a handy number, you should think about it,' I suggested.

'No I'm not gonna keep doin' it,' Dean stated somewhat assuredly.

'You've done it before?' First he seemed to indicate that it had been a spontaneous event.

'Yeah. I shagged her a few times, you know... but she's really dirty...'

He studied the situation while finishing the joint. 'But it'd be so easy to just bang her after the gig...ahh, I don't know man!'

We looked for something else to do. We passed the dirty lake again and then the library, where more blonde D4 girls stood talking and texting. Soon we were back at the Forum Bar where some sci-fi dudes sat around looking vaguely confused, yet elated.

Is é a d'iarr mo stór orm ligint den ól,
Nó nach mbeinnse beo ach seal beag gearr;
Ach dúirt mé léithi go dtug sí an bhréag,
Is gurbh fhaide mo shaolsa an deoch úd a fháil.

From *An Bonnán Buí* (Cathal Buí Mac Giolla
Ghunna)

Translation:
My darling asked me to let the drinking go,
Or else my life will be cut short;
But I told her she made up the lie,
Taking a drink is what lengthens my life.

The Tic Tac Incident

Ciaran had been gorging himself on Tic Tacs all weekend. Although these brightly coloured sweets were first launched in the Summer of Love of 1969, Ciaran was not giving out any love. It was the Irish summertime, and under the most uncertain skies in the world, we braved the grimy campsites of the Electric Picnic.

Ciaran was a mischievous sort and rather than eat the damn things he decided to throw them at people. A few of us were standing around drinking beer, waiting for a band to start. I had a full glass of beer which I had just paid through the nose for and was guarding with my life. Ciaran attempted, from a distance of about three metres, to throw a Tic Tac into said beer.

His first few attempts were so poor that it was clear he was not a sportsman. I had been anxious at first, that he might land one on target, but then laughed and suggested he would be better off eating them. Then, to my horror, he succeeded in landed one in my beer, making a tiny plop sound.

Ciaran stood around laughing, very satisfied with himself. As the glass was full, I had no way to get the little mint out. It began to sizzle furiously and a line of bubbles rose continuously to the top. I decided to make the best of a bad situation and began searching for girls.

I casually approached some festival ladies and expressed my shock and horror at finding a tablet in my beer. It was a conversation starter. Some girls were sympathetic in advising me not to drink it but to get another, others just laughed and kept going. A hippy type girl appeared and I relayed my shocking story. Her eyes lit up.

'You lucky fecker,' she enthused. 'Can I have it? Have you got any more?' I had to come clean.

'It's a Tic Tac.' She was disgusted and walked off with her head drooped.

Finally things improved. The next group of girls were moved by my woes and completed with each other for my attention. I took full advantage and extracted maximum sympathy. One of the girls began to move in and success was within grasp. Then Ciaran, who had been watching my endeavours from a distance, stepped forward.

'It's just a Tic Tac!' he revealed, shaking the packet of mints. 'Don't listen to that chancer!'

The girls were shocked at my brazen duplicity. They informed me that, indeed, I was a chancer and off they popped. Ciaran bellowed with laughter once again as they walked away from my sad gaze. Again he stood around very happy with himself.

He saw no advantage in conducting chit chat with random girls for my benefit. The concept of 'wing man' was lost on him. I rebuked him but he merely replied: 'I was trying to annoy you. You weren't meant to profit from it!' With friends like these...

Out from many a mud walled cabin eyes were watching through the night
Many a manly heart was beating for the blessed morning light
Murmurs rang along the valley to the banshee's lonely croon
And a thousand pikes were flashing by the rising of the moon

From *The Rising of the Moon* (John Keegan Casey) as performed by Luke Kelly and The Dubliners

The Barman

The drinks arrived. Robbie the tall, dark barman had the air of being a nice regular guy. He gave the personal touch when serving the stout. He took the twenty Euro note and was back moments later with the change. His customers, two girls in their early twenties with beer bellies, watched him go back the bar. Like men they commented on him, and nodding to each other, both agreed that they'd like to get into a bed with him at the next opportune moment.

The Brian Boru was a comfortable North Dublin city bar, the kind that had a mixture of hard set local types and flashy blow-ins from the country. I sat at the next table with my flatmate Tommy, an out of work stoner. We had been sitting there for a few hours when Tommy revealed that he had an interview coming up at this very bar.

Back at the flat a few days later he informed me that he'd been in to see the manager. Knowing his character, he would hardly have mentioned it unless he had gotten the job, but I played along.

'How did you get on?'

'Starting tomorrow,' he replied using an economy of words.

'Wow! Well done, man! What time?'

'Half ten. I have to find some clean jocks to wear.'

He went back into the sitting room and picked up where he had left off, smoking joints of bad Dublin hash. The clean jocks would have to wait.

After work a few days later I came home to find Tommy on the couch stoned with Led Zeppelin playing loudly in the background.

'How's it going?' I asked.

'Not bad,' he answered looking hazy. 'Day off.' He took a puff of his joint and rolled his eyes to indicate how good it was.

'Feckin' day off and I'm almost out of smoke,' he sighed despondently. 'Do you know anyone selling hash?' I shook my head.

The following day I found him in the same position on the couch.

'Off again?'

'No. Split shift. Back at 9.'

I sat down and zoned out seeing he had little to say.

'I have some dope coming,' he mentioned.

'So you found someone?'

'Robbie's dropping it down.'

'Who's Robbie? Do I know him?'

'Robbie from work.'

I wondered would he give the same personal touch when delivering the hash as he did with the stout.

*

Two hours later Robbie arrived clad in black jeans and a hoodie. It was the first time I had seen him out of his work clothes. He sat restlessly on the couch, uncomfortable in every position.

The other flatmates were impressed that such a popular guy he had come round and made a sort of fuss of him which he detested. Robbie sat forward; his hands trembled. From his pocket he produced some tiny pieces of bad Dublin hash and placed them on the coffee table.

'Which one do you want?' Robbie asked. Naturally, Tommy took the biggest one and asked how much it was. The answer was not popular and sent his eyes wide.

'Is it that much, yeah?' was his feeble protest.

He was going to pay it even if it was twice that much.

'Yeah,' said Robbie shortly evidently sick of the same stupid questions every time. Tommy paid him somewhat reluctantly. I already knew he would be moaning about this all night.

Robbie's hands still trembled and to ease them he began to roll a joint with yet another piece which he'd produced from his pocket. He rolled and smoked still looking anxious. He was a bit of a strange guy away from work. While at the bar he was always courteous and pleasant with the customers, never looking inward as he was now. When the joint was smoked he got up suddenly dispensing only ephemeral goodbyes.

A few weeks passed and Tommy held onto the job and began spending a lot of time with his new dealer slash work buddy. They were always smoking together after work or on days off. Robbie became Tommy's regular dealer and frequently dropped by with marginally larger pieces of bad Dublin hash.

One day Tommy managed to stop

getting stoned long enough to bring a girl out to dinner. It was quite an achievement in the circumstances. As my girl knew his girl, he decided to make it a double date to take the pressure off. We went to the local Italian restaurant, a North Dublin business which specialised in overcooked pasta and undrinkable wine.

We had struggled through our main courses when the waiter arrived with the dessert menu. Tommy wanted to go for a pint but he had to wait for the girls to peruse and chatter excitedly over the almost exclusively chocolate-based menu. His phone beeped and after reading the message his expression grew dark and troubled.

'Aisling, I've no time for dessert, I have to go.'

She looked at him with surprise. He had already gotten up from the table so there was little she could do to stop him.

'What's wrong?' she asked.

He wouldn't reveal any information, instead threw some notes on the table. He left his girl with a slice of chocolate cake and a confused-looking expression.

Over the next few days he wouldn't discuss anything to do with that evening and I knew not to press any further. Finally the following week he came clean:

'I got a message from Robbie that night asking me to come over to his place immediately...'

It emerged that since Robbie had been dealing bad Dublin hash for a few weeks he had recently managed to increase his market. He needed to buy in bulk and so had gotten a few 9 bars from a dodgy source. These were hardened criminals apparently and not to be messed with.

To make it worse he had gotten the drugs 'on tick,' a helpful arrangement for the small-time dealer which allowed him to sell some or all of his drugs before repaying the supplier. Quite a smart business model in theory but while it works for the wholesalers selling tiles or cement, it doesn't work the same way with bad Dublin hash. You can't smoke tiles or cement. Robbie had either not sold the drugs, or did some bad 'on tick' selling of his own, probably a combination of both.

The heavies had been in contact with our helpful local drug dealer for payment. He hadn't got it of course, so they gave him an ultimatum: get it by tomorrow or we'll come over and kick your head in. They would be over at 9 apparently.

He had gone to a friend's house to lay low. Robbie's unsuspecting flatmate answered the door and was immediately pushed aside as three large angry men burst in swearing loudly. The flatmate got a few clips round the ear to 'encourage' him to reveal the location of their debtor. They left with no money but said they'd be back soon.

Robbie had sent a text to Tommy that night in frightened desperation to ask for help. When Tommy came rushing over he was told the details and was then asked for six hundred Euros to pay off the wholesalers. Evidently Tommy liked Robbie and apparently valued having a cool drug dealer buddy, so he waltzed down to the cashpoint and withdrew the six hundred. That was, coincidently, the maximum daily ATM withdrawal from most Irish bank accounts.

Robbie promised to repay as soon as he sold the drugs. Next day Tommy went to work interested to see how Robbie had gotten on with the heavies. Robbie didn't turn up; he never contacted the bar again or told anyone that he was leaving Dublin.

A few weeks later Tommy heard that he'd gone back to Sligo to lie low. He wondered if Robbie might one day answer some of his calls or messages. He wanted his six hundred Euros back.

'He's gone to England,' was the next update to the continuing saga of Robbie the barman and occasional dealer.

'I'll bloody kill him if I find him,' said Tommy. He never found him.

Is cuma cad é atá i ndán domh
Ag Dia amháin atá a fhios ag sin
Ní bheidh mé choíche cráite
Le buaireamh ná brón
Ach cuirfidh mé mo dhóchas
I nDia mhór na Glóire
Is dhéanfaidh Sé mo threorú
Sa bhealach seo 'tá romhainn

From *An Bealach Seo 'tá Romhainn* (Traditional)
as performed by Clannad

Translation:
It doesn't matter what is in store for me
With God alone is the knowledge of this
I won't ever be riddled
With worry or unhappiness
But I will put my hopes
In the Great God of Glory
He will guide me
In this path that's ahead of us

Unwanted Rural Return

Somewhere in rural Ireland:

'Man, I hate coming home for Christmas,' I said to whomever who would listen. I was here now and I'd better enjoy it, a voice in my head told me.

I'd had a torrid time avoiding the fiends while endeavouring to 'throw' pints of Guinness into me in the small redneck bars. Finally I reached the nightclub, the only one in the town.

There were many villains around, all home from God-knows-where: Dublin, London etc. Lots of faces looked out of place. It seemed as if a crowd of Dublin city hipsters had been transported to a rural setting, put in alongside the local folk, who have to live here the rest of the time, and let mingle. Those who had moved away and those married to them all circulated amicably, exuding twice the personality and confidence of the assembled locals. They were easy to spot. The locals hated them.

I went to the toilet and stood pissing, lost in thought. Would it be worth my while to take that job? Should I try that almost inaccessible bird at the bar? Just then someone gave me a box in the mouth. I was mid-piss and I sprayed wildly. I had to cut it off, not easy for a man, and find out who the hell was this bastard who had just cold called me. A bearded unrepentant fool stood beside me with his dick in his hand. 'I'll scriss you,' he said.

'Come again?' I asked. He evidently meant me further harm.

I got out of the toilet while he was still pissing. He was giving it a shake as I left. I ran into Tommy, a villain of the highest order, and told him the gory details. The short corridor that led to the toilets became overcrowded with impatient revellers with full bladders.

We both stood in anticipation when eventually the fiend emerged in his bastard bearded glory.

'Who do you think you are, hittin' this man?' Tommy asked the fool.

'He started a fight with me down the disco. I was giving him the slap back,' said the bastard.

'I've never seen you before in my life,' I declared.

'Ahh...,' he said then, 'I made a mistake. I hit the wrong man.'

He thought that would be enough to let it pass. He'd then go slap some other fiend that looked like me but maybe wasn't. He looked at Tommy. Tommy gazed back with eyes devoid of any feeling. The fool got spooked but decided to fight his way out of another corner. Without notice he swung around karate style to trip Tommy, but he didn't fall. The fool looked yet more foolish. Tommy smiled soullessly.

'Ahh, that didn't work did it? You're not as quick as you think you are.' Others pushed us en route to the 'jacks' uninterested in our petty squabbles.

'Who are you anyway?' he asked us. We told him the truth, as to tell a false name in a small town such as this could have the entire mob on your back. We posed the same question to him.

'I'm Matty Farrell. I'm one of the Fighting Farrell's from Cootehill.' We looked at him incredulously. 'I'm home from London for the Christmas.' We held back the laughter for a moment, then let loose. There would be no fight; this guy was too much of an idiot. He was a symbol of amusement. He saw his chance to get away and bowed a respectful bow to the pressure of Tommy and left with only childish menace left in his actions. Licked like a fool, he left.

*

A few days later and still suffering the toil of a trip to that horrible town I waited for the 'round the world' taxi trip home. The taxi driver would pull up in his minivan and take whoever got in first. When the van was full he would ask everyone where they were going before making a route plan. Of course many were going in conflicting directions. He might have 3 people going northwards; a few to the south of the town, and a few living quite close by. Unbeknownst to some he would be planning to drop them home last.

He would typically start out the road in the opposite direction of where you had to go and keep going for half an hour or so. When he finally turned back towards the town he would ask you again where you wanted to go. This ray of light kept your hopes up for a while longer. When he arrived back in town he would again stop and pick up more passengers who might actually want to go in the same direction as you had just come from. No matter, he would take them the 5 miles or so home before turning back towards town a second time. Then once more he would ask the people aboard where they wanted to go. You would repeat yet again your destination upon which he might send you to another taxi, that of his colleague who would be back in a few minutes from the Shercock road.

You were back on the street again now one hour later, back exactly where you had started. You had to again wait for a taxi and hope you might be first on so as to ask the driver to go your way. It may happen that the driver had not intended to go your way and you had been 'misinformed.' 'I'm sorry,' was the only consolation given and again you had to wait on the street. When at last a taxi came that genuinely promised to take you home you rejoiced.

A few nights after my nightclub experience, I was in one such 'round the world' taxi going home from town. The driver was the same man who used to drive the school bus back in the days of toil that were the 90's. He told me that he would be going my way but first he had to drop home this fine young man who sat in the front seat. His passenger was a drunken farmer who sat snoozing for most of the journey, far from a fine young man. When Pete the driver asked me the immortal words: 'How did you get over the Christmas?' we got on to the experience in the nightclub.

'I was there taking a piss and some guy just smacked me out of the blue. I never saw him before and I've no idea why he hit me. Anyway you don't hit a man while he's having a piss.'

'Who was he? Did you find out?' asked Pete. The country mentality reappeared.

'Yes, he said like an eejit,' and I affected a deplorable accent to illustrate, 'I'm one of the Fighting Farrell's from Cootehill!'

Just then the drunken farmer awoke from his whiskey slumber.

'Who the hell are you?' he asked. 'Where are you from?'

As I mentioned earlier, you have to tell someone the truth in these situations, it is an unwritten rule. 'I took that man over from London,' he said angrily. 'He's a good friend of mine, who the hell are you to be saying things about him? I'll fucking *scrios* ya!'

There it was again, that old Gaelic verb pronounced 'scriss,' that those involved in fighting talk apparently exuded on occasion. It could have been 'D'ya wanna buy a dag?' it was all the same. The fiend wanted to *scrios* or I presume, destroy me. He had to be restrained by the frightened taxi driver who told us that he would rather take us home alive. He looked at me with the kind of rage that might have been directed at cattle rustlers had they ever operated in the depths of Ireland.

'The taxi's not the place for fighting,' said Pete.

The fiend relented.

'Only you're in the taxi. Only for the taxi, I'd *scrios* ya!' Ambling out of the car, the half animal then lurched down the driveway to his house where he still lived with his parents despite being 35 and a semi-professional drunk.

'Take me home,' I urged Pete who had seen many a similar fiend attempt to 'scriss' me on the school bus years before. Don't pick up any more people on the way back through town (for the third time), I hoped. Leave the small town, leave it to the savages who bawl and howl like madmen. Leave it to them and never visit.

Enjoyed Back to the Gaff? Why not leave a review online.

Want to find out more about John P Brady?
Check out his website:
www.johnpbrady.com

Roadside Fiction formally published a free quarterly online literary magazine. Ten issues of material are archived online. For more info on Roadside Fiction publications visit our website:
www.roadsidefiction.com